Castaways & Longer Days

TRIXIE SILVERTALE

Sittin' On A Goldmine
Productions L.L.C.

Sittin' On A Goldmine Productions, L.L.C.

info@sittinonagoldmine.co

www.sittinonagoldmine.co

ISBN: 978-1-952739-06-4

Cover Design © Sittin' On A Goldmine Productions, L.L.C.

Trixie Silvertale
Castaways and Longer Days: Paranormal Cozy Mystery : a novel
/ by Trixie Silvertale — 1st ed.

[1. Paranormal Cozy Mystery — Fiction. 2. Cozy Mystery — Fiction. 3. Amateur Sleuths — Fiction. 4. Female Sleuth — Fiction. 5. Wit and Humor — Fiction.] 1. Title.

CHAPTER 1

THE WARM SUMMER air around Pin Cherry Harbor sparks with the electricity of a celebration. For the past two weeks, I haven't had a single conversation about anything other than the Midsummer Regatta and Bonfire.

As I walk down Main Street, the usually calm scene is rife with activity. They've tied summer bunting around every streetlamp, and the partially abandoned downtown area has transformed into a summer wonderland. Groups of tourons, who've driven up from the big cities far to the south, are meandering down the street pointing, smiling, and taking an inordinate number of selfies.

Myrtle's Diner overflows with patrons and enticing aromas. You have to wonder how the owner can keep it all straight! When I enter, I'm surprised to receive my standard spatula salute through the red-Formica trimmed orders-up window as though it's a slow Tuesday in January. My dearly departed grandmother's first husband, Odell, runs the diner and also serves as my surrogate grandfather. As I approach he nods toward the counter, and, as if by magic, another local slides from her stool and lays some cash next to her plate.

I'd recognize that five-foot-tall bundle of energy anywhere. "Hey, Artie, I never did ask what keeps you busy in the summer. Even this far north, there's no snow to plow in June."

We share a friendly chuckle and she reaches out to pat me on the shoulder as she passes by. "Oh, the city keeps me real busy, don't you worry." Pointing to my T-shirt, she grins. "The sheriff make you wear that?"

My blue tee sports an indifferent cat and the tagline: Coffee, because murder is wrong. I paint my features in a portrait of innocence, fluff my snow-white hair, and reply, "I'm sure I don't know what you mean, Artie."

Her knowing nod calls my bluff. "Will I see you at the celebration today?"

Not the first time I've fielded this question today. I nod emphatically. "I wouldn't miss it."

She dips the brim of her baseball cap and politely pushes her way to the door.

I hastily drop my ample backside onto the vacant seat before it disappears.

Almost-Canada's best waitress slides a glorious cup of java across the counter to greet me. "Mornin', Mitzy. You headed down to the harbor?"

Part of me wishes I could secretly watch the chaos from the fire escape at the back of my three-story bookshop, but I've lived in a small town long enough to know that participation in such a massive community effort isn't optional. So I opt for the standard local response. "You betcha. Bell, Book and Candle sponsored one of the sailboats in the race, and we provided all the wood for the bonfire on the beach."

She raises the pot of fresh-brewed coffee in her age-spotted hand and makes an impromptu toast. "Well, you be sure to take an umbrella, in case that storm hits." She rolls on with her salutation before I can ask my burning storm-related questions. "It's true what they say about you. You're a good influence on this town, Mitzy Moon."

I lift my mug of black gold and nod. "I think it's the other way around, Tally."

She winks and spins on her oil-resistant shoes. Her tightly bound flame-red bun bobs happily as she moves through the restaurant, filling coffees and tending to her customers.

Odell sets my breakfast in front of me, raps his

knuckles twice on the silver-flecked counter, and hustles back to the kitchen. The glorious scent of scrambled eggs with chorizo and golden-brown home fries immediately lifts my spirits and erases any lingering rain worries.

With more patrons queuing up by the minute, I waste no time in cleaning my plate and downing a second cup of liquid alert.

As I step away from the counter, Odell nods his utilitarian grey buzz cut and I head back to the sidewalk to make my second stop of the morning.

The Pin Cherry Harbor sheriff's station is a cross between the one featured in *Roswell* and the homespun headquarters in Mayberry. Oh, their training is up-to-date, their firearms have the latest bells and whistles, and their interrogation rooms contain video surveillance. However, the rest of the place is straight out of the 1950s. Wood-grain paneling, a swinging wooden gate that hangs askew, a typewriter on every desk, and deeply scarred wooden chairs next to each dented metal homage to law enforcement history. But I don't come here for the décor. I come here for the *sights*.

Rounding the corner into the sheriff's office, I lean against the door, kick out a hip and grin, in what I hope is an inviting way.

"Well, if it isn't the famous local sleuth, Mitzy Moon." Sheriff Erick Harper drops the file he was perusing, and rises to his full six feet and change. He runs a hand through his slicked-back blond hair and smiles warmly. "Better get over here and pay your fine before I double it."

Happy tingles flip-flop through my tummy as I stride forward into his embrace.

His warm hugs always make me feel safe and protected.

"What? No tax?" I widen my grey eyes and offer him a sip of my sass.

The glow of new love rapidly heats up his small office, and I can't remember ever feeling more foolishly blissful.

He curves around me and leans down to plant an inappropriately delicious kiss on my eager lips. Before things have a chance to bubble over, we receive an unwelcome interruption.

The AM/FM radio perched precariously on Erick's ancient file cabinet wails out an emergency alert beep followed by an urgent message:

The National Weather Service has issued a
* Severe Thunderstorm Warning for . . .
All of Birch County . . .
The City of Grand Falls in central Birch County . . .
The City of Round Rock in northern Birch County . . .
The City of Pin Cherry Harbor in northern

Birch County . . .

    * Until 330 PM CDT.

    * At 900 AM CDT, a severe thunderstorm was located near Thief Falls, and near Pine Lakes, moving east at 30 mph.

HAZARD . . . 65 mph wind gusts and quarter size hail.

    SOURCE . . . Radar indicated.

    IMPACT . . . Damaging winds may cause some trees and large branches to fall. This could injure those outdoors, as well as damage structures and vehicles. Roadways may become blocked by downed trees. Localized power outages are possible. Unsecured light objects may become projectiles.

My heart races for the wrong reasons and I lean into my boyfriend's broad chest. "Should I be worried?"

He nuzzles into my neck and whispers. "Not with me around."

Someone clears their throat loudly, and I turn my blushing cheeks toward the door.

"Excuse me, Sheriff. There's a permit snafu that needs your sign-off."

The portly and persistently agitated Deputy

Paulsen fills the width of the doorway. As usual, her right hand rests on her gun and her gaze reeks of schoolyard bully.

Come on, you know me. I have to poke the bear. "Good morning, Deputy. Are you working the bonfire detail?"

She sighs loudly. "I'm the Coast Guard liaison."

I wait for further explanation, but clearly that simple phrase is meant to impart all the knowledge needed.

Erick squeezes his arm around my shoulders and answers the many questions he knows are pinging in my snoopy little brain. "Paulsen is making sure all the boats taking part in the parade and regatta are permitted for the event, and aren't over capacity. She'll be down at the marina checking permits against the entrant list and the Coast Guard will manage illegal speed infractions and run the DUI checks on the water."

"The what now?" My head tilts to the side.

Erick laughs. "I keep forgetting you grew up in the deserts of Arizona. Driving while under the influence of alcohol or illegal substances is just as unlawful on the water as it is on the road. The Coast Guard takes that very seriously."

I nod and click my tongue. "Boy, you learn something new every day in this town."

Deputy Paulsen grumbles, and her pudgy hand

flinches as she re-grips her gun. "Sheriff, the permits."

"10-4. Give me one minute, Paulsen."

She scoffs, as though she doesn't believe he can keep me to time limits. "10-4, Sheriff." Unfortunately, as soon as she waddles back toward her desk, the vacancy is instantly filled by Deputy Candy.

In case you've forgotten, he creeps me out. He's supposed to be some kind of genius, and he's barely eighteen. However, on each of our previous run-ins, he's been quite forward with me. Erick thinks I'm exaggerating, but—

"Morning, Mitzy. I like those jeans." His eyes linger.

See what I mean! Ew. Thankfully, Erick answers for me.

"I'm sure you didn't come in here to compliment my girlfriend, Deputy. What do you need?"

"Just signing out with you, Sheriff. I have that elite surveillance training course this weekend. Unless you need me to stay in town?"

Erick playfully tickles my back as he slides his arm from my shoulder and walks closer to Deputy Candy. "Nope. Got everything handled. Go take your course and be prepared to give a presentation to your fellow deputies when you return." He reaches out his hand, they shake firmly, and Candy departs.

As he turns toward me, I open my mouth to complain for the millionth time about Deputy McLeer-y. He raises his finger to silence me and nods his head. "I heard it that time. No need for your protests. The kid definitely has the hots for you, Moon. Take it as a compliment."

"I'd rather not." Shaking my head, I reach for his hand. "I have to get back to the bookshop and help Twiggy set up the solstice display. Are you sure I shouldn't be concerned about the possibility of this storm turning into a tornado or something?"

"Ask anyone. The lake has its own microclimate. I've been sheriff for nearly six years and I've never seen a tornado make it this far north. They always peter out around Grand Falls." He offers me a reassuring smile.

Mmmmm, that kissable pouty mouth. Mentally scolding myself, I do my best to return my focus to the conversation. "Will I see you later?"

He squeezes my hand and smiles. "Of course. For some reason, they assigned me to monitor the sector from the cul-de-sac at the end of Main Street, along the harbor, all the way up to Pancake Rock. Can't imagine how that happened."

I open my eyes wide. "So you'll be patrolling all around my bookstore today?"

He kisses my cheek, and I blush. "See ya later,

Moon. I better go take care of these permits before Paulsen blows a gasket."

"Copy that."

The crowds are spilling from the sidewalks directly onto the street now, and as I walk to my bookshop on the corner of Main Street and First Avenue, the white peaks of several pop-up tents catch my eye. Never let it be said that the residents of Pin Cherry Harbor miss an opportunity to courteously separate tourists from their money.

Each vendor is selling a different irresistible item. The booth closest to my store is festooned with pre-made floral wreaths. I've been told multiple times how all the girls, and even some of the boys, adorn their heads with these wreaths for most of the day, and, during the bonfire, toss their summer circlets into the great lake to carry the wearers' hopes and dreams to fruition.

Having grown up in Sedona, Arizona, I'm familiar with the idea of manifestation. In the Southwest, we deal primarily in vortexes, crystals, and other airy-fairy conveyances. I honestly never paid much attention to it.

Of course, that was before I rode an odiferous bus for forty plus hours and discovered the ghost of my not-as-dead-as-everyone-thinks grandmother living in my bookshop!

Not to mention the added bonus of my super-secret psychic powers, which continue to surprise me with new and expanding functions.

I would happily buy a flower wreath, but I've been informed, in no uncertain terms, that I must weave my own wreath if I sincerely desire my dreams to come true when I toss it into the chilly waters of the enormous lake nestled in our harbor.

There are two booths selling different variations of Pin Cherry Harbor souvenirs and T-shirts, but it's the final vendor who has my full attention. Individual strawberry cakes!

Oh boy! I'm absolutely going to buy one immediately, and I thoroughly believe I'll be back more than once later today.

I queue up in the small line to purchase a scrumptious cake. The strawberries on top glisten beautifully, and I think the presentation would impress even our local patisserie owner.

It takes every ounce of the self-control I don't possess to keep from shoving the delicacy directly into my mouth. With my luck, I'd trip on nothing and offer the crowds a priceless photo op when I face plant into the whipped cream. Best to take calming breaths and wait until I'm inside my store.

Pausing a moment to admire the one-of-a-kind, hand-carved door that graces the impressive entrance to my inherited bookshop, I squeeze my shoulders together happily and rush inside.

CHAPTER 2

I BARELY MAKE it three strides before a familiar voice barks from the back room. "If you're carryin' one of them cakes, and I know you are, you can put it straight in the mini fridge."

The chill of guilt slides across my shoulders. How does she know? It's truly inexplicable. My volunteer employee, Twiggy, either has eyes in the back of her head, or secret spy cams planted throughout the bookshop.

She was my grandmother's best friend in life, and, at some point since my arrival in this tiny town, I managed to impress her enough to win her over. She won't let me pay her for her contribution to running the bookshop, but front-row seats to the many disasters of my life seem to be compensation enough.

Defiantly, I sneak a juicy strawberry into my mouth and, as predicted, instantly stumble over *nothing* on the carpet, nearly dropping my entire cake!

A rich, low cackle echoes from the back. "If you drop that cake on the freshly shampooed carpets, I'll quit this instant."

"Calm down, Miss Bossy Pants. Everything's just fine." Lucky for me! I'd be lost without her, but I'd never admit it. "Hey, I thought Stellen was going to help us set up. Where is he?"

"Apparently you missed a family memo, kid. Your stepbrother has his advanced orientation weekend at the university down south. Your dad said they were all going to spend the night in the dorms and everything."

My heart twists with a flicker of pain. I love my stepbrother, and I'm excited that my father and his new wife are accompanying him for his maiden college experience. However, growing up an orphan, flowing in and out of a variety of foster homes, there's a part of me that aches with jealousy. No one came to my postgraduate facility to wish me luck. Maybe if they had, I wouldn't have dropped out less than a year later.

Although, you'd be surprised how much a person can learn in eight months of film school. I had a real knack for cinematography, and I'm sure more than one person would tell you that my natural bossiness would've lent itself nicely to a career in directing.

But that path was not to be. I dropped out and chose to receive my education at the school of hard knocks, and the lessons were plentiful.

When my grandmother's attorney, Silas Willoughby, who also happens to be a masterful alchemist, found me holed up in my hovel in Arizona, I'm sure he thought he'd made a wrong turn.

Life as a broke barista had not been kind to me. So when he handed me a large envelope filled with cash, a mysterious key, and a promise of a new life, I was sure some student filmmaker had unwittingly cast me in their magnum opus.

I'll never forget the uncertainty that flooded through my body when I took my first step onto the sidewalk in Pin Cherry.

Initially, I was sure I'd made a horrible mistake, and, if not for the flickering neon sign announcing Myrtle's Diner and the irresistible call of the fries, I may have gotten right back on the bus and never discovered this amazing place.

"I need to run upstairs and get Grams. I promised her I'd wear her all day today. She's extremely eager to be part of the ceremony."

Twiggy slowly turns her office chair toward me

like a day-old dessert rotating in a glass pastry case. "Is she still trapped in that necklace thingy?"

"Yep. That cursed amber pendant the gypsy used to trap Grams' ghost is proving a bigger puzzle than Silas hoped. He's supposed to get back tomorrow from that extended visit to his brother's. I can only hope he found some kind of solution. I think Grams is going a little stir crazy."

Twiggy shakes out her sharp salt-and-pepper pixie as she nods. "Myrtle Isadora was never one to be tied down."

We share a knowing chuckle. My grandmother was a firebrand in life and nothing changed after she left this plane, and, through a series of carefully planned alchemical transmutations, had her soul bound to this bookshop.

Unfortunately, a gypsy with a grudge and an ancient magical tome uncovered a means to trap my grandmother's soul in an amulet. She can no longer float about the bookshop at will, or scare the bejeezus out of me by popping through walls. However, she can still eavesdrop on my private thoughts. She splits her time between hanging in the closet, which I've nicknamed *Sex and the City* meets *Confessions of a Shopaholic*, or dangling around my neck.

Of course, she'd prefer I wear the pendant 24/7, but I had to insist on some privacy.

Circling up the wrought-iron staircase, I reach the Rare Books Loft and inhale deeply. The subtle smell of old books, dusty secrets, and magical worlds holds my attention for a moment.

The beautiful solstice sun is shining through the double-stacked rows of large six-by-six slumped-glass windows that grace the front of the store. The tin-plated ceiling glows silver-blue, and tiny dust motes float and drift like miniature fairies attending to the stories hidden within my vast collection.

I drag a finger across one of the oak reading tables, but no dust exists on the surface. It's all floating through the bookshop, casting an air of mystery.

Adjusting the green glass shade atop the closest desk lamp, I smile inwardly at my newfound sense of responsibility. I've developed a genuine pride of ownership.

This is my bookstore, and I love every inch of it. Reaching up, I pull the candle sconce that serves as the secret handle activating the bookcase door, which slides open to reveal my hidden apartment.

Bookstores, ghosts, alchemists, and secret doors. This is a life I never dreamed existed back when I was shoving my belongings into a black trash bag and shambling off to yet another foster situation.

"Mitzy? Is that you?" Her voice is thick with anxiety.

"Calm down, Grams. It's absolutely me, and I've had my private meeting with Erick, so I am ready to put you on."

"Thank heavens! Pyewacket disappeared hours ago and I've been alone up here, absolutely losing my mind!"

The news that my fiendish feline has vanished is hardly noteworthy. The half-wild tan caracal comes and goes as he pleases. If he wants something, he'll let you know. And if you're ever lucky enough to scratch his broad head between his black-tufted ears, consider yourself in the company of a rare and precious few.

"I think you should wear the white sundress. It's perfect for a solstice celebration."

"Are you kidding me? It's windy as a mountaintop out there, and everyone's talking about some kind of storm. I'm not gonna get caught in a sudden rainstorm in a white dress! In case you don't remember, we try to keep it PG around here, Isadora!"

Grams giggles uncontrollably, and I remove the pendant from the hook in my massive walk-in closet. As I secure it around my neck, she breathes a sigh of relief. "I feel better already. You have to wear something summery, though. You can't be running around the festival in skinny jeans!"

"I'll tell you what. You let me keep the skinny

jeans, and the comfortable shoes, and I'll allow you to pick out any top you like."

"If I could take corporeal form, you wouldn't be able to push me around like this."

"And if wishes were trees, you'd live in a forest. Do you want to pick out the shirt or not?"

She groans as though it pains her to acquiesce. "Fine. But when Silas gets me out of this chunk of amber, you're gonna get your comeuppance, young lady."

Sliding the pendant back and forth on the chain, I whisper, "Maybe I'll call him and tell him to spend another week at his brother's."

"Well, I never!"

We both giggle uncontrollably. And, in my mind's eye, I can still see her elegant ghost dressed in vintage silk-and-tulle Marchesa, with diamonds adorning her fingers, strands of pearls around her slender neck, and, of course, tears of joy trickling down her cheek.

"Oh, Mitzy. You know me so well!"

"Yes, I do. And that's why it shouldn't surprise me, that, despite my many reminders, you continue to drop in on my private thoughts—uninvited. If I've told you once, I've told you a thousand times: just because you can, doesn't mean you should. Get out of my head, woman!"

She chuckles wickedly and my shoulders slump in defeat.

"Take me over to that section of blouses on the far left, sweetie."

"I'm going to regret this, aren't I?"

She squeals with excitement. "See that red top, with the spaghetti straps?"

"Unfortunately, yes."

"Pull it out and take a gander."

Sliding the hanger from the bar, I turn the top back and forth. "It's a little sexier than I was imagining, but I like the color."

"It will look fabulous on you. I can't wait to see."

I whip off my snarky T-shirt and carefully pull the top over my head. Twisting left and right in the full-length mirror, I grin. "It's cute. I think I actually like it."

Placing my foot up on the padded mahogany bench, I strike a silly catalog pose.

Grams can see my reflection in the mirror and immediately giggles. "That should catch Sheriff Harper's attention."

"Easy, Grams. I've mastered the attention-capturing part. Now I have to figure out how to keep it. That's where my relationship experience always runs into trouble. My usual pattern is to rush in blissfully trusting, but wake up alone shortly thereafter."

"Well, Lord knows you took your time with this one. If it takes you half as long to extract yourself from this relationship as it did for you to make an actual commitment, you've got at least six months of good times ahead."

The color drains from my face. I drop onto the bench and reach for the pendant with my left hand.

When the mood ring on my finger comes in contact with the amber gemstone, my entire body buzzes strangely and I let go of the stone. "I don't want six months, Grams. I want forever. Or at least as close as I can get to it."

Contrary to her usual behavior, Grams remains silent.

"Grams? You don't have anything to say about that?"

"Mitzy, is there an image in the ring?"

The question comes out of left field, and I'm not sure how to answer. On all previous occasions, the ring has either gone icy cold or strangely hot before it delivers an image. I release my hold on the necklace and glance down. There's a nondescript image of debris floating on water.

"That was weird."

"What do you mean, dear?"

"I didn't get any chills or tingles. What made you think there was going to be an image?"

"Gosh, I'm not sure. I might've had one of my premonitions. I haven't had one since I've been trapped in here. How odd."

"Copy that. I better remember to tell Silas when he gets back. You know how he is about reporting even the subtlest things."

We share a chuckle at his expense, and I pop into the bathroom to put a little sunscreen on my shoulders. Yet another disadvantage of spaghetti straps.

While I'm hard at work applying the SPF 50 to my bare shoulders, my cell phone pings.

Flipping it over, I read the ALERT:

Tornado Watch Number 417 - Storm Prediction Center 1130 AM CDT

The Storm Prediction Center has issued a

* Tornado Watch for portions of

Birch County . . .

The City of Grand Falls central Birch County . . .

The City of Round Rock in northern Birch County . . .

The City of Pin Cherry Harbor in northern Birch County . . .

* Effective this Saturday morning and evening from 1130 AM CDT until 530 PM CDT.

* Primary threats include . . .
One or more tornadoes possible
Scattered damaging wind gusts to 80 mph likely
Isolated large hail events to 1.5 inches in diameter possible . . .

That sounds serious. "Grams, maybe we—"

"Oh pshaw. I lived through more tornado seasons than I care to count, sweetie. Pin Cherry has always had the protection of the lake, and today won't be any different. The skies are blue and the storms are way down south."

Before I can offer a counter-argument—

CHAPTER 3

AN EAR-SPLITTING BOOM pierces the silence, and a puff of smoke rises over the harbor.

The resulting cheers and screams of delight lead me to believe it's something good, not bad. What if—

Grams squeals. "It's starting! Get going, Mitzy."

Good to know. The horrendous sound was the official start of the Pin Cherry Harbor Midsummer Regatta and not whatever a tornado sounds like.

She continues to urge me along as though I'm her Kentucky Derby mount as I race down the stairs and out the side door, into the alley.

When I reach the shore behind the bookshop, I'm pleased I made the correct exit choice.

The cul-de-sac on the other side of my bookshop overflows with folks from all the megacities down south. The smell of sunscreen, fried treats, and strawberry cake wafts over me. The visitors and locals have spilled over the seawall, down the steep escarpment, and onto the beach. Flower-wreath-topped heads are sprinkled across the grass and sand all the way to Pancake Rock, and they're all cheering for their favorite boats.

A sleek array of wind-powered vessels skims across the harbor like waterborne rockets. Bright summer sunshine glistens off the waves and a surge of shouts follows the ships as they whisk past the distant pier and head in our direction.

I'm pleased to see Sheriff Harper's fine form on scene as he checks the first-aid tents set up along the shoreline.

Personally, I'd be more inclined to peek in on the vendors offering smoked salmon, new potatoes and dill, more strawberry cakes, loose flowers, or possibly even the stand offering pre-made wreaths. I suppose that's why he's the professional and I'm the *amateur*.

This far north of the equator, there's an almost cult-like reverence for summer solstice. The obsession is surely fueled by the short growing season for crops and those who believe the brief window for sun-related fun is a subject to be celebrated.

Having survived my second winter in this

quaint town, I absolutely get the appeal of warm weather.

An area adjacent to Pancake Rock has been roped off with buoys and declared an official swimming hole. I'll keep my distance, though. My last jaunt to the stacked flat rock outcropping did not end well, but that's another story.

The grassy slope transitions abruptly into the sparkling sand and smooth-pebbled beach behind my bookshop, where this evening's bonfire will roar to life. As an official sponsor of the event, I'm duly impressed by the sheer height of the conical tower of stacked wood.

The mini mountain of driftwood collected by local scout troops complements the generous donation of old pallets from my father's railroad.

Teetering atop the pinnacle is a beautiful wooden sun, carved by a local chainsaw artist. They have declared it the official town offering of the festival. A fairly generous gift, considering his works usually sell for a minimum of nine hundred dollars apiece.

I wave at Erick, and he gives me an official head nod. Yes, our relationship is out of the closet, but when he's on the job, he's all business. He looks very handsome in his summer uniform. Despite the humidity, he refuses to allow the deputies to wear shorts, but he gave in on the short-sleeved shirts. His muscular bare arms already show early signs of a promising farmer's tan, and his blond hair is sure to lighten under the intense solar attention.

"Mitzy, honey, take me down by the water so I can see the boat race."

After the initial shock of hearing Ghost-ma's voice, I recall having placed the haunted necklace around my neck. It's unusual for her to be quiet for so long, and I honestly forgot she was here. "No problem. I'm on it."

I thread my way through the sizeable crowd with a series of friendly shoulder taps and excuse mes—eventually making it to the water's edge. The coarse sand gives way to a swath of polished pebbles under the crystal clear water.

Without thinking, I step forward to grasp a glistening heart-shaped red agate. Surprise! I still have my high tops on.

Now they're squishy wet, but it actually feels kind of refreshing and I did get the awesome stone. Sliding it in my pocket, I shade my eyes and take in the final leg of the regatta.

A long blast from the deep throaty foghorn on the island signals the winner has passed the lighthouse.

The crowd cheers wildly as a voice crackles over the public announcement system. "Your solstice regatta winner is Flouncy Flouncy!"

And, as if they had perhaps some psychic sense about the outcome, the Fergie song, "Glamorous," bursts to life over the speakers and eager summer celebrators get jiggy with it.

A boat horn honks in the harbor, and all heads turn.

Wouldn't you know? Leticia Whitecloud has chosen to insert her casino boat directly into the middle of the festivities.

Down at the pier, a line is already forming, and I'm sure Leticia will be only too happy to ply her patrons with alcohol to ensure their bets are hefty.

The horn toots two more times as she passes the beach, and the crowd eagerly responds.

Ever since that woman had me kidnapped and tried to hold me for ransom, I've disliked her greatly. Maybe it's her involvement in the majority of the area's illegal gambling, off-track betting, and dishonest shenanigans in general. The regional Tribal Council ousted her last year, but her power runs deep. She somehow remains a dark influence in the native gambling scene. Charges never seem to stick, and this floating casino is one of many loopholes she oozes through.

Grams exhales with disgust. "She's a dangerous piece of work, dear. I can't believe she's here."

Clenching my jaw, I mumble my reply. "Not

my problem, but at the same time, I'll keep an eye on her."

Shoot! I ran out of the bookshop so quickly I left my strawberry cake in the mini fridge. Not to worry, I'll simply buy another one and perhaps a glass of strawberry wine to wash it down.

"I'd rather you skipped the wine."

"Seriously? I'm not an alcoholic." Frustration laces my boisterous objection.

Nearby heads turn and expressions range from confused to judgmental.

Oops! I suppose I should avoid speaking out loud to my grandmother's ghost when surrounded by strangers who can neither see nor hear her. Time to institute telepathic communication.

Grams, I respect your struggles with alcohol and I'm glad you found support through Alcoholics Anonymous, but I'm not an alcoholic. However, in the spirit of family love, I'll skip the libations today. And I'm lifting the ban on thought-dropping while we're at the celebration.

"Oh, goody! I've been biting my tongue so hard it would surely be bleeding if I were alive!" She sighs dramatically. "You have to buy some loose flowers and weave your crown."

That statement makes me laugh out loud. *You know, I've always thought I needed a crown.*

Grams giggles. "It must run in the family!"

Finishing my new strawberry cake and my paper cup of ice tea, I approach the flower stall hesitantly.

The joyful dark-haired woman behind the table smiles warmly. "Happy solstice! You look like a lady who needs a crown!"

I chuckle and nod. "Clearly my reputation precedes me."

The lady running the booth doesn't quite get my humor, but she offers another hearty smile nonetheless. "Do ya know what kind of flowers you want?"

"No idea. Does it matter?"

Out of the corner of my eye, I observe a young girl shove a bunch of daisies under her stained T-shirt. "I think daisies are probably the easiest to work with. I'll take a bunch, and I'm paying for hers too."

The obsidian-haired girl turns white as a sheet and gazes at me with a heavy burden of guilt pressing down on her petite shoulders.

"That will be ten dollars, and we only accept cash."

I realize the vendor has to say that for the sake of the tourists, but I've been around long enough to know better than to attempt using plastic at an event like this. After all, Pin Cherry Harbor is officially the town that tech forgot. Cash is king everywhere.

The gangly girl-child attempts to sneak away during the brief financial transaction.

"Hey, bunch of daisies, I think you owe me an explanation."

She stops and her shoulders sag in despair.

I catch up to her and soften my tone. "Look, I'm no goody two shoes. I totally understand if your parents can't afford to buy you flowers."

She shakes her head but keeps her eyes trained on the ground between her dirt-streaked bare feet.

"If it's not a money thing, why are you stealing?"

She shrugs and refuses to look at me as the wind swirls her long, tangled hair.

"Well, if you're not willing to cooperate, I'll have to call the sheriff over and see if he can get the truth out of you."

Her head pops up and her eyes widen with fright as she blurts, "My mom doesn't know I'm here."

My head tilts with concern. "You mean, she doesn't know you're at the flower booth, or she doesn't know you're at the Midsummer Festival?"

The girl grips her bunch of daisies tightly to her chest. "Both."

Hunkering down to her level, I proceed with

my casual chat. "My name's Mitzy Moon, and I own this bookstore behind us."

Ghost-ma pipes up. "Go easy on her, Mitzy. We all had a reckless streak in our youth."

Ignoring my self-appointed guidance counselor's interruption, I continue. "I think you better start at the beginning. Because, frankly, what you've told me so far is a little alarming."

She nods and continues to grip her bouquet snugly. "My name's Chayce, and I'm nine years old. My mom promised to take me to the festival, because it was gonna be her weekend anyway, but she didn't show up this morning."

There are no tears springing to the corners of her dark-brown eyes. I'm no expert, but I'd say this isn't the first time her mother has disappointed her. "And your dad couldn't bring you?"

"Nah. He had to work at the airport today."

"So you're here all by yourself, with no adult supervision, and your parents don't know where you are?"

She rises on her tiptoes and shakes nervously. "You won't tell the sheriff, will you?"

Placing a friendly hand on her shoulder, I lean in and whisper, "Let me tell you a little secret. The sheriff happens to be my boyfriend. So, if you promise to show me how to weave these flowers into a wreath, I'll keep you out of trouble."

The fact that young Chayce made no mention of a babysitter spikes my concern level up a few notches. She's clearly smart, responsible, and industrious, but she also suffers from a child's lack of discernment. Sadly, I'm all too familiar with the poor judgment of youth.

We thread our way through the crowd to the shade of a large white cedar, and she shows me how to make a daisy chain.

"I wonder which came first? The flower wreath or the computer network?" The girl turns a confused face toward me and tucks a strand of blowing hair behind her ear. She appears to be indifferent to my clever quip.

However, Grams lets out an amused snort.

Hairs tingle on the back of my neck and I turn my head to gaze at the horizon to the south. The dark grey storm clouds have visibly thickened, and an eerie shade of yellow tinges the sky.

The brisk winds, which have been whipping my hair into my eyes all day, abruptly cease.

Phones all around me PING simultaneously.

Out of nowhere, Erick races toward me. "Tornado! Everyone has to take cover now!"

I don't need to look at my phone. Shouts of, "Tornado emergency!" echo through the crowd.

A familiar ghostly voice cuts through the din.

"Mitzy, you have to get as many people into the storm cellar as possible."

"We have a storm cellar?"

Erick looks at me. "Are you asking me or telling me?"

Oops, I did it again.

Ghost-ma continues shouting instructions. "At the back of the bookshop there are two large steel doors on the ground. Erick can help you open them and you should be able to fit at least two hundred people inside. There's no time to waste, sweetie."

Erick hesitates a moment longer. "Mitzy, I have to make decisions about people's safety. Do you have a storm cellar or not? The tornado has already touched down and at the rate it's moving, it will be here in seventeen minutes—or less."

"Yes. I think so. Behind the bookshop."

He races in the direction I'm pointing, and I blindly follow.

The sight of an angled cement-block-sided mound, partially overgrown with ivy, shocks me. Apparently, I have a storm shelter.

A disaster siren screams out a warning, but that is old news. We know the tornado is coming and the added wail only serves to increase general panic levels.

Erick rips back the vines and grips one of the

huge handles, but the doors won't budge. "They're locked! Where's the key?"

The look on my face isn't the answer he wants.

Desperate to please him, I'm about to employ the special alchemical trick Silas showed me for opening locks. Lucky for me, fate has other plans.

"Sheriff, I've got the key right here." Twiggy is puffing her way toward us in her biker boots. Surprisingly, she's moving at quite a clip for a woman her age.

She kneels on the doors, shoves the large key in the lock, and it clicks open with a satisfying thunk.

Erick grabs one door, while Twiggy and I pull together on the second. The huge doors screech against their rusty hinges and fall open, and Erick immediately hits the button on the microphone clipped to his shoulder. "This is Sheriff Harper. The storm cellar behind Bell, Book and Candle is open. Direct everyone south of Pancake Rock toward me. Situation report. Over."

The various deputies acknowledge from their posts throughout the festival, and information about other shelters follows.

Erick climbs up the fire escape ladder to the platform and shouts instructions to the terrified festival attendees.

Twiggy and I wave our arms wildly to draw attention to the shelter entrance and help people down the stairs as they approach. She calls instructions to the first occupants for how to turn the lights on, and a steady stream of people rush to safety.

The crowd is thinning rapidly, and a wave of relief washes over me when I realize there is room for everyone.

The beaches are empty, and the violent storm winds have doubled their ferocity. They're already overturning the pop-up tents and scattering souvenirs and first aid supplies into the water.

Erick swings down from his perch. "Got to make one more pass around the building and look for stragglers. You and Twiggy get in the shelter. And close one door."

"Copy that."

As he turns to leave, an agitated man in a reflective neon-orange vest races around the corner. "Sheriff! I can't find my daughter. I left her at home this morning, when I went to work. They closed the airport, so I went back to the house. My ex-wife said she never picked her up, but my daughter's not at the house. I just know she came down here on her own. You've got to find her!"

Before Erick can reply, I shout over the rising wind. "Is her name Chayce?"

He nods anxiously. "Have you seen her?"

"Yes. She was right here in this crowd. She's probably already in the cellar."

He runs past me, down the stairs, shouting his daughter's name. Word spreads quickly through the refugees, but there is no "Chayce" in the shelter. His horror-stricken face surfaces. "She's not in here."

Without thinking, I make a promise I pray I can keep. "I'll find her. You stay safe."

He attempts to follow, but Erick talks him down, closes one door, and follows me as I run wildly toward the beach, calling the little girl's name.

"Mitzy, you need to calm down and use your powers. It's your only hope. You've only got minutes to find her, sweetie."

Grams is right. I stop and take a deep breath. The white-capped waves crashing onto the sand are already twice my height. It's difficult to stay focused in this environment.

"Mitzy! What are you doing? Get away from the shore. Those waves are gonna reach twenty feet or more before this is over. You've got to get in the storm cellar."

Shaking my head fiercely, I step back. "I'm not going in until I find her."

Erick's whole body quakes with exasperation, but he knows me too well. "Fine. Any hunches?"

As soon as he asks, something spikes through the chaos and I can see her trapped under one of the overturned tents. I mean, it's not like I actually see her; it's more like heat vision. Must be a new power, because I've never experienced it before. "There. She's under that tent."

Erick and I rush forward, and he lifts the damaged canvas structure while I reach my hands under to pull the girl free. "Come on, Chayce. Your dad's waiting in the shelter."

"Is he mad?" Her little voice shakes.

I hug an arm tightly around her shoulders as I hunch and run forward. "No, sweetie, he's not."

We hurry down the stairs, and she dives into the open arms of her father. All I can think is how glad I am that I found her, and how doubly glad I am that my dad is safely on a college campus with my stepbrother, and nowhere near this disaster.

"I couldn't agree more." Grams' voice is thick with emotion.

Erick pulls the door shut just as a giant limb from the enormous white cedar crashes to the ground inches from the shelter.

The earth shakes around us, and the wind is deafening.

Everyone huddles together in a fearful hush.

Torrential rain thunders down, but is quickly drowned out by the howling scream of the tornado.

CHAPTER 4

IT HARDLY TAKES a psychic to sense the height-
ened fear of everyone huddled in the shelter. You
can smell the dread in the air. The six dim bulbs
seem to hold the only flicker of hope as I gaze out
over the sea of anxious faces.

The storm rages on outside our safe haven.

Erick grips my hand firmly while he checks in
with the other deputies. Reports of twister touch-
down sightings and damage are flooding in.

And then—the lights snap out and we're all
plunged into darkness.

Several choked screams rise from the throng,
and a few children cry.

Sheriff Harper continues to clasp my hand
tightly, and I feel his protective instincts swell as he
takes a deep breath. "Please remain calm. It's likely

that the power will not come back on. Once the storm passes, we'll open the doors and you will all be able to exit safely by the light of day. Please stay put. We don't want to risk anyone getting hurt by moving around in the dark." The authoritative, confident tone of his voice belies his racing heart.

Murmurs of agreement rise from the crowd, and I'm proud of my kindhearted, levelheaded guy.

Once the shrieking winds pass and the staccato beat of the deluge lessens, Erick initiates another round of updates from the deputies positioned throughout the area. "Situation report."

Deputy Johnson confirms clear visual on the dissipating cyclone. "Yes, Sheriff. Once it hit the water it pulled up a spout at least fifty, maybe a hundred feet in the air, but then it spun itself out just as quickly."

"10-4." Erick slides his hand from mine and squeezes my shoulder as he stands. "Folks, we have confirmation that the tornado has blown itself out. There is significant damage and debris along the tornado's path. In addition, there are power lines down along that same corridor. When you exit the storm shelter, please turn right at the top of the stairs and proceed to Main Street. There are no live power lines down along that route, but there will be debris and broken glass. Proceed with caution, and anyone who is concerned about leaving the shelter is welcome to stay as long as they like. I have to get out there and organize the rescue efforts."

He turns to heft open the door and a man's voice calls out. "Sheriff Harper?"

"Yes, sir, how can I help?"

"Do you know what happened to the boats in the regatta?"

Erick draws a ragged breath. "We'll see for sure when we get out there. But it's my understanding that several boats capsized and I'm sure some sank. The Coast Guard will be picking up survivors."

In the darkness, a collective gasp temporarily swallows all sound. But the brave man has more to say. "Well, if it's all the same, Sheriff, I've got a boat and I'm more than willing to head out there and grab as many as I can get on board."

Before Erick can answer, several more voices call out in the darkness.

"Same here, Sheriff."

"Count me in."

A little tear spills from the corner of my eye. Maybe they've been through a tornado before, but it is the single most terrifying storm I've ever experienced. The fact that these generous people have the wherewithal to think about rescuing others warms my heart and lifts my spirits.

"Thank you. All of you." The sheriff thrusts the

door open like a blockbuster hero, steps out, and yanks the second door back.

The occupants of my storm cellar calmly file out, waiting patiently for their turn and helping those in need.

A handful of folks choose to stay in the shelter, and I offer to find them some bottled water. When I emerge from this opening in the earth beneath my bookstore, my heart nearly stops beating.

Gazing toward the once pristine lakeshore, I turn my head left and right. The landscape is unrecognizable.

The scent of raw, overturned earth is heavy in the air. Huge shards of glass, plastic lawn chairs, parts of wooden picnic tables, an upended stroller, scattered flower wreaths, and so much trash!

I've never seen such destruction. Running toward the alley, I glance up and am relieved to see the bookstore and my father's Restorative Justice building intact.

Erick catches up with me. "Glad your store is okay. There are a lot of people in trouble. I may not see you again for a couple of days. Drink only bottled water, and hopefully they'll get the power back on before we all starve." He smiles wistfully, kisses me, and rushes off toward Main Street.

"Mitzy!" The familiar little voice brings a smile

to my stunned face. I turn toward Chayce and her father.

"Thanks for finding my little girl. She tells me your name is Mitzy Moon. I can never repay you, Miss Moon."

"Call me Mitzy, and you don't owe me anything. Chayce here already taught me how to make flower wreaths. In exchange, I told her I'd keep her safe. That was our deal."

The little girl grins for a moment, and then the corners of her mouth turn down. "I lost my daisies."

"I tell you what. Once we get the power back on and make sure everyone's safe, you come visit me at the bookstore and I'll make sure you get a whole basket of daisies."

Her eyes light up. "For reals? You promise?"

I take my pointer finger and trace an "X" over my chest. "Cross my heart and hope to die. Plus you'll get to meet my furry—"

Grams and I shout in unison, "Pyewacket!"

"Sorry, Chayce, I've gotta go. I have to make sure my cat is all right."

Without waiting for a response, I race down the alley and into the bookshop.

"Pye? Pye, are you in here?"

Nothing.

I lean against a bookcase and force my breathing to slow. Reaching out with all my psychic senses, I struggle to find even a shred of his energy.

I feel nothing.

I hear nothing.

I see nothing.

And the only things I know for sure are a hellacious twister visited almost-Canada and my precious fur baby is missing.

Cut to—

Reaching up with a heavy arm, I pull the sconce that serves as the candle handle opening the sliding bookcase door.

Nothing happens.

I pull it again.

Nada. Bupkus.

"Grams! What the heck? The bookcase won't open."

"The power is out, dear." Her tone is matter-of-fact.

"I'm aware. How do I get in?"

"The emergency crank."

Waiting for further instruction proves fruitless. "And . . .?"

"Oh! This must be your first power outage. I didn't realize. Head down to the cupboard under the stairs, where we keep the luggage. There's a panel at the back that pops open to reveal a pulley and crank system. It's been a while, but I think you turn it to the right to open the bookcase and the left to close. You'll figure it out, sweetie."

I'm sorely tempted to unhook the chain on the stairs. If there's no power, the alarm can't possibly sound. However, knowing Twiggy, she has a secret backup battery for the alarm system. I don't want to divert important rescue efforts with a false alarm.

The powers that be bless my crossing. Made it!

Using the light from my phone, I locate the panel in the small angled closet at the back of the children's books section and start cranking.

A welcome scraping sound thunders above my head as the bookcase door slides open. Hooray for ingenuity!

The search intensifies as we move methodically through the shop.

One and a half hours later, Grams and I have searched every square inch of the bookstore, printing museum, and my apartment.

There is no sign of Pyewacket.

However, cell phone service has finally been restored and my father called to say he's on his way back to offer whatever help he can. Amaryllis and Stellen are staying at the college for the rest of orientation week.

I fire off a text to my stepbrother to let him

know we're all doing well, and I wish him an exciting week at the university. Notably, I omit the news about my missing wildcat. Stellen has a heart as big as Texas when it comes to animals, which is why he wants to become a veterinarian. If I mention anything about the missing caracal, he'll come sailing back and miss out on his once-in-a-lifetime experience.

Granted, I'm not pleased that I can't locate Pye, but I have faith in the furry fiend, and I believe he'll find his way back to me.

The good news is that my bookstore escaped any serious damage. There are at least six cracked panes of glass in the many windows on my three-story shop, but none smashed through, and, so far, no water leaking inside.

While I wait for my dad's return, I take a cautious stroll through town to see if I can lend anyone a hand. Before I head down Main Street, I make one last pass down the beach.

Vendors are busy collecting trash, folding up any awnings that can be salvaged, and retrieving their damaged wares. A multitude of personal watercraft and small private boats bob along the choppy surface of the great lake, searching for survivors.

It looks like any local with a serviceable flotation device has joined the rescue efforts. Reports of fourteen capsized sailboats and five additional missing vessels have come in through the local gossip chain. The big news, however, is that Leticia Whitecloud's floating casino capsized and sank like a stone! I can't say I'm sorry, but I do hope everyone escaped safely before the ship went down.

Main Street is littered with cardboard, paper, small branches, and lightweight plastic items. I haven't seen the exact path the tornado took, but it would appear this section of town was spared any serious damage.

Popping into the diner, I'm shocked to see lights on and smell food cooking. "Odell, how do you have power when no one else on Main Street does?"

His deeply lined face tilts up from the grill, and his sharp eyes lock onto mine. "I may have been billeted a cook in the Army, but that doesn't mean that's the only thing I know how to do. I keep a generator on site, with enough fuel for a week, and I test it annually."

"Copy that. I should have known you'd be prepared."

"Do you need something to eat, kid?"

His question produces an odd reaction. Never in my life have I not known the answer to that query. But the events of the day have thrown my body's natural rhythms so far off course, I can't remember the last time I've eaten, and I don't know if I'm hungry.

Odell's raspy chuckle eases my concern. "Listen, you sit down and I'll get you squared away. I've seen that look before. It's shock. You made it through without bumps and bruises, but if that was your first trip to Oz, trust me when I tell you you're in shock."

I wouldn't dream of questioning my surrogate grandfather. I slide onto the red-vinyl bench seat, place a hand on my stomach, and both hear and feel its growl. Hooray! One thing has returned to normal: I'm hungry.

Moments later, Odell places a plate of chili cheese fries in front of me with a bottle of water.

"Thank you! This is exactly what I need right now. Comfort food and hydration." Downing a huge glug of water, I wipe my mouth with the back of my hand and smile. "Being so prepared and all, you wouldn't happen to have a spare case of bottled water, would you?"

He slides onto the bench seat opposite me and grins. "I notice you're wearing that necklace again. I'll make you a deal. You tell me the story behind that piece of jewelry and I'll give you *two* cases of water."

Gulp.

"You can't tell him, Mitzy. He won't be able to

see me or communicate with me. It's too much. It'll just upset him. You can't tell him!"

Searching the recesses of my brain, I attempt a subject change. "I only need one case. I had six bottles in my mini fridge, and I gave those to the folks that wanted to stay in the storm cellar. But if you can spare a case, that'll get me through a couple of days, and I can give them each a bottle for the road."

He sits back and narrows his gaze. His lined face speaks of age, wisdom, and an intolerance for malarkey. "There's something odd about you avoiding my question. Is it stolen?"

For a moment, I toy with the idea of fibbing, but his intense stare tells me I'd be a fool to try. "The truth is, I came by it honestly. I can't speak for its provenance, but I like wearing it."

My vague answer brings a crooked grin to his clean-shaven face. "Fair enough. A deal's a deal. I'll grab that case of water." He raps his knuckles twice on the table and disappears through the kitchen.

"Whew. That was close," I whisper.

Grams sighs mournfully. "He's the kindest man. Maybe I should've stuck it out. I was so young and impulsive. I suppose I was just a stupid old quitter."

"Don't say that. If you had stuck it out, you never would've met Max and decided to get sober, and most of all, you never would've married Cal and had my dad. I wouldn't be here!"

Odell pauses next to the old pushbutton phone on the wall. "Are you talking to me, kid?"

Yeesh! Get it together, Moon. "No, I suppose the pure joy of eating these delicious chili cheese fries is making me speak in tongues."

He chuckles as he sets the case of waters on the table. "Let me know if you need anything else. Feel free to send folks down here if they need something to eat. I reckon the Piggly Wiggly got themselves a generator or two after the last ice storm took out the power for a week. You should be able to purchase anything else you need there, as long as you have—"

"Cash!" We utter the punchline simultaneously.

He grins and saunters off. Powering through my chili cheese fries, I bus my dishes, and lug the case of waters back to the bookstore. All but three of the refugees have exited the shelter. "Do you folks need more water?"

"Thanks. We're good."

"All right. If you're hungry, the diner on Main Street has a generator and they're serving customers."

That announcement is all it takes. The remaining trio hurries to the top of the stairs.

"Which way?"

"Around this corner of my shop and straight up Main Street. It's on your right-hand side. You can't miss it." Listen to me, giving "can't miss it" directions like a local.

"Thanks. Do you know if the airport has reopened?"

"I don't. But I'm sure the owner of the diner has all that information."

The out-of-towners nod their thanks and creep forward with extreme caution.

Inside my bookshop, Twiggy is up on a ladder taping over the cracks in the panes of glass.

"You don't have to do that. My dad's on his way back and he said he'd help us board up the windows until we can get the panes replaced."

"Don't worry about me, doll. Some of these cracks are dangerously close to giving way. We definitely don't want the rain, that's sure to be pushing the rear of this storm, to drip through, or, worse yet, blow out a window and ruin a whole section of our inventory."

"Understood. Do you need any help?"

Despite the day's disaster, she cackles loudly. "I've seen you on ladders before. If you managed to survive a category five tornado, I don't want your death on my hands!" Her raucous laughter continues.

"Rude." I mumble under my breath as I stomp

up the treads of the circular staircase toward my apartment.

Grams is unable to control her giggling. "What is it that you always say?"

"No thought dropping? Get out of my head, woman?"

"No, no. About being wrong."

"Oh, you're not wrong."

Grams snickers loudly. "That's the one. She's not wrong."

My snark kicks into overdrive. "And what is it you always say, Isadora? Well, I never!"

The momentary distraction passes, and the sharp pain of my missing mascot hurts my heart when I see the bookcase door standing open. Grams and I decided to leave it open until the power is restored, but the sight reminds me of my missing furry friend.

Approaching the raised section of paneling beneath the built-in bookcase inside my apartment, I press firmly and step back as a secret, spring-loaded drawer pops out. From the drawer, I retrieve a pendulum and a folded map of Pin Cherry Harbor.

"Oh, what a great idea, dear."

"Yeah, I won't be able to sleep tonight without knowing what's happened to Pyewacket."

Grams inhales sharply. "Me neither."

"That's not really the same thing, Grams."

"Well, I'm just as worried about Mr. Cuddlekins as you are."

"No doubt." Smoothing the map open on the coffee table, I drop into the scalloped-back chair usually reserved for Silas.

"Silas! I got so distracted by the storm and searching for Pyewacket, I totally forgot about Silas."

"But, I thought he wasn't due back until tomorrow?"

"I know, Grams. I'm sure he heard about the storm, though. He probably couldn't get through because the cell service was out for so long."

Before Grams can offer any other hypotheses, I pull out my phone, dial Silas, and hit the speaker icon.

"Thank goodness. I was worried sick about you."

Between you and me, the way I can verify the depth of his concern is that he abandoned all etiquette and asserted his concern without first offering a proper greeting. "Well, good afternoon to you too, sir."

He chuckles, and I can picture his round belly and heavy jowls jiggling as his face reddens. "It is apparent you survived the tornado with your wits intact."

"I did. The only thing that isn't intact is Pyewacket—"

"How dreadful! Has he gone to meet his maker?"

Grams screams her protest.

"Settle down, Grams. I'm sure he's all right."

Silas harrumph's loudly. "You should retrieve your pendulum—"

"Already doing it. My mentor taught me well. Now hurry up and get back here, so we can get Grams out of this infernal amber!"

A lengthy pause causes me concern. "Did I lose you? Are you still there?"

"I am here. My brother and I may have devised a solution. However, our endeavors to undo the gypsy's curse must wait until the town is restored. Have you heard about the library?"

"First I'm hearing of it, Silas. What happened to the library?"

"Sadly, the reports I've heard describe a dismal scene. The tornado laid waste to the entire structure. Buildings a block away, on either side, remain basically unharmed, but our beautiful library is no more."

My bookshop and all of my precious tomes have become such an important part of my life. The thought of the library's destruction brings tears to my eyes. "Is there anything we can do? Can we salvage any of the books?"

"I'm scheduled to arrive late this evening, and we may visit the site together tomorrow. Perhaps there is some assistance the Duncan-Moon Foundation can offer. That remains to be seen."

Mournful silence hangs between us.

"I shall see you tomorrow, Mizithra."

Oh brother. Not the formal name. Anything but that. "Safe travels, Silas. Wish us luck in finding Pyewacket."

"He will not require luck. Robin Pyewacket Goodfellow makes his own fortune."

CHAPTER 5

Extending my right arm above the flattened map, I let the pendulum drop and wait for the chain and conical stone to find plumb.

Pressing my left hand to my chest, I take a deep breath and attempt to locate my own center. Without warning, the amber pendant I'm wearing starts to levitate.

"Grams? Grams, are you doing that?"

"Doing what, sweetie?"

"The stone—the cursed stone—it's floating!"

"It is? I was trying to be quiet and focus on finding our beloved Pyewacket. I can't explain the—"

Thud.

The stone drops to my chest and an odd flutter ripples across my skin. "Whatever you were doing, try not to do it again. It's super distracting. I need to focus to use this pendulum thingy."

"I'll do my best, dear."

Shaking out the willies, I start over and hold my question firmly in my mind. "Where is my beloved —our beloved—caracal, Robin Pyewacket Goodfellow, right now?"

Handled. I think I covered all my bases and kept my question specific enough to avoid getting a misleading result. I wish Silas were here to pull a mysterious vial from his tattered tweed jacket and give me the answer I need.

The pendulum vibrates, arcs once counterclockwise, spins clockwise twice, and pulls firmly toward the location of the Bell, Book & Candle on the map.

I drop the chain in disgust, jump to my feet, and press a hand to my forehead. "It's obviously broken! We searched this place from top to bottom. There's no way he's in the bookshop!"

"Try to stay calm, Mitzy. Shake off your doubts and try again."

"It's not the doubts that are getting the best of me, Grams. It's the certainty that something terrible has happened. Silas promised me Pyewacket had at least three lives left. I take that seriously. You know?" Emotions are boiling over. I need to tamp down this torrent of *feels*.

"I understand, dear. Mr. Cuddlekins means the world to me, too. Let's take a deep breath and try again."

I drop onto the overstuffed settee, exhale loudly, and pick up the pendulum. Rolling my shoulders back a couple of times, I inhale a lung-expanding breath and form my question again. The pendulum quivers—

BANG. BANG. BANG.

"What the—?"

"Language, Mizithra! It's only someone pounding on the side door. The bell isn't working, remember?"

Dropping the pendulum onto the map, I stumble across the Rare Books Loft and trudge down the stairs toward the metal door under the not-glowing-red EXIT sign leading to the alley.

My voice brims over with frustration as I open the door and snarl, "I was right in the middle of some—"

"Any chance this belongs to you?" Broad-shouldered, ice-blond, Jacob Duncan stands in my alleyway with a smirk on his face. But the sight of my father is not what brings tears gushing from my eyes.

"Pyewacket!" Grams and I shout in concert.

I lunge forward and scoop the beast from my father's arms.

"Take it easy on him, Mitzy. He has a nasty cut on his chest."

The massive feline is too large to be cradled like a baby, so I step inside and gently place him on the floor, while I crouch to examine his wound.

"There's goopy stuff in it."

"There is. As soon as I found him huddled in the corner of my garage next to a broken window, I called Stellen to see if I needed to take him to the vet."

Tears continue to trickle down my cheeks as I scratch Pyewacket between his black-tufted ears. "Oh shoot, I didn't want Stellen to worry."

Jacob chuckles. "He wasn't worried at all. He said Pyewacket was a tough old kitty, and I put him on speakerphone so he could talk the beast through the cleaning procedure he was recommending."

My fingers stop their scratching, and I gaze up at my father. "And Pyewacket let you clean the cut and put the goop in there?"

"He did. But all that was thanks to your step-brother. And that *goop* is aloe vera gel. One hundred percent organic and safe to be licked by his royal furriness. The cut is superficial, thankfully."

Grams is whispering syrupy sweet nothings to her precious. It's so over the top. My dad is lucky he can't hear her.

"We have several broken windows over at our

place. I'm going to get those boarded up before we run out of daylight, and I'll come by and help you tomorrow. Sound good?"

"Honestly, Dad, if bringing back Pye was the only thing you ever did, you would've already exceeded all expectations."

"Hear! Hear! Tell him how happy I am." Grams is crying and continuing to coo to her favorite guy.

"Grams is at least as thankful as me, if not more so."

My dad nods his head and steps back. "You're both welcome. Let me know if you need any grub. Amaryllis stocks up on canned food like any day could be the next apocalypse." His laughter follows him across the alley and I shout one last thank you as he disappears into his building.

"We were so worried about you, son! What were you doing in dad's garage?"

My normally sassy cat takes the silent approach and lovingly licks my hand.

"Don't ever scare us like that again. I could learn to live with losing this whole bookshop and everything in it—except you."

"Reow." Can confirm.

"Oh, the little sweetheart feels the same way about you, dear."

"Wow. I feel a bout of stress eating coming on hard. Today was too much. I'm going to indulge in some unhealthy snacks and see if Dad wants to join the rescue efforts tomorrow."

Grams clicks her tongue. "There may not be anyone to rescue tomorrow. The lake is deep and dangerously cold, even in June. Flotation devices will help keep heads above water, but it's the hypothermia that's the real danger."

"Why am I only hearing about this now? If that's really the case, I'm leaving you here with Pyewacket and I'm going to go see if Dad wants to get out on the lake right now."

"Oh, Mitzy, it sounds too dangerous. You should wait until morning."

"No way. You said yourself, there may not be anyone to save by morning. I was fortunate to come out of this unharmed and with my home and business intact. I think I owe it to the community to do something with that good fortune. Don't you?"

"I'm sure you're right. I just worry."

After fielding additional protests from my overprotective Ghost-ma, I position Pyewacket in the middle of my four-poster bed with an extra pillow supporting his large head.

"There are bowls of Fruity Puffs and water right here on the floor if you need them, buddy. Just rest. I'll be back before you know it." I place the amulet containing my grandmother's ghost on the summer comforter next to the reclining feline. "You both be good. See you in a few hours."

Using my key, I let myself into the Duncan Restorative Justice Foundation. I'm met with the rhythmic pounding of a hammer echoing from outside, and a surprising amount of shattered glass strewn across the lobby around the feet of the statue of my late grandfather, Cal.

Looks like my dad's building took the brunt of the high winds edging the tornado's track.

The best path forward seems to be backward. I retrace my steps to the alley and jog out to the sidewalk along First Avenue. "Hey, Dad. Can you come down a minute?"

He gazes over from the top of his ladder and removes a handful of nails pinched between his lips. "Let me finish hammering up this piece and I'll be right down."

Pacing across the mouth of the alley, I again take in the panorama of the storm's damage. The inordinate volume of paper blowing through the streets like two-dimensional tumbleweeds sends a pang through my gut. Upon first inspection, I assumed all the paper debris was trash. Now that I've learned the fate of the library, the horrible realization hits me: the shattered remains of the thousands of books in the city's collection are now nothing more than litter.

Silas wants me to accompany him to survey the damage tomorrow, but I'm honestly wondering if I'll be able to stomach it. The clomp-scrape of my father's work boots on the rungs of the ladder pulls my attention to the present.

"What's going on? Did you decide to take me up on that offer of food?" He smiles warmly and pokes the handle of his hammer through the loop on his tool belt.

"Actually, I was wondering if we could take the boat out and help with the rescue efforts?"

His eyebrows rise, and he leans back. "Rescue efforts? I have to be honest, Mitzy. When I heard someone mention a tornado touched down in Pin Cherry, I jumped in the truck and hurried home. The radio doesn't work in that old thing, so I didn't hear how bad things were. Of course, I can see the destruction, but what rescue efforts are you talking about?"

"The twister hit during the parade and regatta. Tons of boats capsized, and some even sank."

My father wipes a worried hand across his brow. "Holy cow! I had no idea. I'll toss this tool belt in the garage and we'll hit the road. The *Tax Sea-vasion* is docked in a slip at the marina now that I sold the old Duncan place. There's no telling if the storm left her seaworthy. The waves must've been out of control."

"I didn't see the worst of it. Erick said they might hit over twenty feet high as he rushed me into the storm cellar, so no visual confirmation. I'm kinda glad I didn't see it. It sounded terrible."

Walking and talking, we jump in the old 1955 Ford F100.

The road down to the marina isn't clear, but my dad manages to blaze a trail through or around the debris. A jetty on one side, and the isthmus leading to the tribal casino on the other, protects the marina. A few small boats appear banged up, but as we approach the Duncan family yacht it bobs in its slip unharmed.

"I'll give her a once over. You get on board and count the lifejackets." He heads down the dock while I hop onto the deck.

"Oh, and Mitzy, make sure we've got plenty of rope!"

"Copy that."

In a matter of minutes, we're underway. The blue sky pushing the clouds eastward gives no indication of the early afternoon's tragedy.

My father gets on the radio and makes a general announcement about joining the rescue effort and our boat's capacity. He barely finishes his "over and out," when a familiar voice comes over the air.

"Good to know, Duncan. I've got twenty-four survivors who found their way to the lodge on

Hawk Island. No hurry picking them up. We have plenty of food and water. We're making a list of names. But there's someone here who needs to speak to you privately."

A dark cloud passes over my father's face.

"What is Nimkii talking about? Who needs to speak with you privately?"

My father shakes his head. "Duncan here. Is it urgent? Would prefer to pick up survivors before dark. We'll head out to the island at sunset."

Nimkii hops back on the radio. "Copy that. Meet me on your dad's channel."

Mention of my deceased grandfather pinches my father's shoulders together with tension. "Switching now. Over."

"What does he mean?"

My father flips a dial on the side of the radio. "My father and Nimkii had a special channel for private conversations. The channel I was on, 16, is used for rescue operations like the one happening today. That way everyone gets the same updates and can pick up any distress calls that might be coming from vessels in trouble."

"And the secret channel?"

He sighs. "In the old days, before the current spotty cell service on the island, they had a system. Nimkii and Cal were great hunting buddies, and they may not have always followed the rules on what was in season. If either of them got a hot tip, they'd notify the other one, switch to the secret channel, and make their plans."

The Native American's voice comes over the radio on the new channel. "Duncan, you here? Over."

"I'm here. Over."

The next voice to sound from the speaker is not the owner of Chez Osprey, but it is familiar nonetheless.

"Jacob? It's Jimmy."

My father looks at me and shakes his head. "What's up?"

"I know you don't owe me anything, but Leticia Whitecloud is missing."

My hand immediately covers my mouth as my eyes widen.

"What happened, Jimmy?"

"Huge waves. Maybe thirty feet. Never seen anything like it. The casino boat capsized before we could get everyone off. I was helping with the lifeboats . . . I lost track of her. I don't know if she made it off the ship."

Jacob bites his lip, and I sense him struggling with his conscience.

"Serves her right, Dad. She's a terrible human being. If you want my opinion, you're under no obligation."

He exhales and wipes a hand over his mouth and chin. "This sounds like something the Coast Guard should handle, Jimmy."

Jimmy's voice is barely a whisper. "What if there was foul play, Duncan? I hear your daughter's some kinda detective."

My hands immediately go to my hips. "As if! His boss had me kidnapped, held me for ransom, and he personally played a part in threatening me that one time out at the casino—"

Jacob presses his lips together and shakes his head. "We have to rise above it, Mitzy. If there's one thing I learned during my fifteen years in the slammer, it's that you never regret taking the high road."

My shoulders sag and I blow a raspberry through my lips. "Why do you have to be such a good person?"

"I have a lot to make up for." He puts an arm around my shoulders and gives me a little squeeze as he keys the radio. "We're making rescue passes while daylight holds. Then we'll pick you up, Jimmy. Over."

"I owe you one, Duncan."

I snatch the radio from my dad's hand and fashion my response. "You're going to owe us both more than one, Jimmy. We'll talk terms when we're face-to-face."

The chuckling voice of Nimkii comes over the

radio. "Sounds like that girl of yours is a Duncan to the core, Jacob. See you when we see you. Over."

The area between shore and Hawk Island is awash with activity. Hundreds of small fishing boats have joined the rescue efforts. Off in the distance, two Coast Guard vessels are moving in concentric squares in the water.

My father steers wide of the official search and rescue operation and slows as we approach a sailboat lying on its side as though it's just taking a nap.

There's no one clinging to the upturned hull, and my non-aquatic instincts immediately turn toward the open water, searching for additional survivors.

"Mitzy, take the wheel. Stay close to this wreck. Circle if you must. I think I see something."

Without waiting for my protest, my father takes off his boots, loops a rope around his waist, and jumps into the water.

A horrified gasp escapes my lungs as I run to the steering wheel. What the heck is he doing?

He pulls himself onto the capsized vessel and moves toward the half-submerged mast.

I still don't see anything.

"Mitzy! Cut the engine! Drop the anchor!"

Just because he's shouting things at me doesn't mean I know how to do it. Cut the engine. Sounds simple enough. I twist the key to the off position and the powerful thrumming stops.

Step one: check.

Now to figure out how to drop the anchor. My eyes quickly scan the various buttons and at last come up with a possible winner. I hit the button and hear the satisfying clunk-clunk-clunk of chain being released. Hopefully, that's the anchor dropping and not the engine!

Hurrying to the back of the vessel, I peer out at my father.

He's found someone tangled in his or her rigging. They don't appear to be alive. When I suggested joining the rescue effort, I kinda hoped to find survivors, not corpses. My stomach is swirling, and it's not from seasickness.

"He has a pulse! Radio the Coast Guard."

For a moment time freezes. My dad's swimming toward the ship on his back, dragging a body that may or may not be alive, and he told me to do something . . . Right! Call the Coast Guard.

"Coast Guard? Come in, Coast Guard."

"Mitzy?" Nimkii offers assistance. "You need to spin the dial back to Channel 16."

Great! More things I don't know how to do. I stare at the dial on the side of the radio and hope that I'm turning it the right way. That looks like sixteen. "Coast Guard. Come in, Coast Guard."

An official voice crackles over the radio. "Go for Coast Guard."

"We found an unconscious survivor. We need medical assistance." Oops, forgot the sign-off bit. "Over."

"Copy that. What's your location?"

I shake the microphone and stamp my feet. How do I know where I am? I'm on a massive lake.

"Hit that large red toggle switch above your head. Tell them you're flashing an SOS beacon from the *Tax Sea-vasion*."

I do as my dad says, and the Coast Guard confirms they're en route.

Meanwhile, my father is diligently performing CPR on the victim.

No response.

It's all too grim. Tears are leaking from my eyes.

Flashing lights and a wailing siren approach. The Coast Guard ship slides alongside, hangs some buoy things over their side, and tosses some kind of grappling hook onto our railing. "Prepare to be boarded."

Despite the awful circumstances, the pirate-y phrase brings a flicker of a grin to my face.

The man on the deck convulses, and my father tips him to his side. The victim vomits up a significant amount of water and gasps for air.

My dad exhales and sits back on his heels.

The Coast Guard personnel lift the man onto a stretcher and transport him to their vessel.

The woman who boarded first shouts back to my father as she releases the hook connecting the two boats. "Good work, sir. You saved a man's life today."

A flash of emotion races across my father's face and spikes my clairsentience with a mixture of relief, gratitude, and bottomless regret.

"What's wrong, Dad?" I hurry to his side and put a hand on his shoulder.

He looks up from his kneeling position and shakes his head. "It just feels like it'll never be enough."

I don't have to ask. I know what he means. They killed an innocent civilian during the course of the robbery he took part in all those years ago. While he may not have pulled the trigger, he'll always carry the burden of guilt. Some people might think saving a life would erase the damage, but that's clearly not how my father sees it.

CHAPTER 6

WE INSPECT THREE more capsized vessels on our way to the island. Thankfully, there are no more bodies. I sincerely hope all the survivors either swam to shore or were picked up by other boats.

Jimmy and Nimkii must've been keeping watch. Two mismatched figures walk down the sturdy dock as we approach: one large and intimidating; one smaller and curved with age.

"Any word on the gambling ship?" Jacob calls out to Jimmy.

He shakes his head and stops beside our vessel. "Permission to come aboard?"

My dad nods and reaches a hand toward the tall, powerfully built man.

Jimmy grasps the outstretched hand with his meaty mitt, shakes it once, and climbs aboard.

Ignoring our new passenger, I address the owner of the lodge and restaurant. "Where are the rest of the survivors, Nimkii?"

The generous man smooths a strand of salt-and-pepper hair back from his lined forehead and tucks it into his long braid. "I'll give the three of you a minute to discuss things. Then I'll send some folks your way. How many, Jacob?"

My father glances at me. "How many life-jackets do we have, Mitzy?"

I'm drawing a complete blank, but I'm calm enough to use my psychic replay to review my memory clip of counting the buoyancy vests. "Twenty-one."

Nimkii nods. "There's a family of five who would be happy to spend the night here. I'll send the others down in about ten minutes." He tilts his head toward Jimmy.

The towering man asks, "Can you make it fifteen?"

He lifts his chin to acknowledge the request and strides back to Chez Osprey tucked under the pines.

Jacob dries his hair with a towel and tosses it on the captain's chair. "I've gotta say, Jimmy, this whole business with the gambling ship really sounds like something the Coast Guard should be handling."

Surprisingly, Jimmy nods. "I agree. I just— I don't think it was an accident."

My dad's face registers pure shock. "You think someone planned to capsize the casino boat?"

Jimmy's powerful neck tilts from side to side, and I can sense him struggling with the truth.

And I pounce. "Look, Jimmy, if you want my help you better be straight with me. As you know, there's no love lost between me and your boss."

He nods slowly. "I understand. She was not a good person, but she was a strong woman. She did harm. I won't deny it. But she helped many people. Fuel oil bills were paid for families in need every winter. And she made sure cords of wood mysteriously appeared on people's front yards when they needed it most. She may not have come by her money honestly, but she made sure her people were cared for."

Crossing my arms over my chest, I narrow my gaze. "Agree to disagree."

Jacob steps forward and attempts to broker a détente. "A lot of ships capsized during the storm. Boats have been skimming across the water all day, picking up survivors. What makes you think Leticia isn't sitting at home in a warm bath with a glass of birch vodka?"

Jimmy puts both of his hands in the air as if

we're suddenly in the middle of a Wild West stickup. "I need to reach into my coat."

My father nods once.

I had almost forgotten the respect Jimmy holds for my father. When my dad was in prison, he took Jimmy's son under his wing. Their sentences overlapped for several years, and Jacob kept him safe while the young man adjusted to survival in the state pen. Even though Jimmy technically worked for the enemy, he always held my father in high regard.

The bodyguard slips his hand in his coat and pulls out a waterproof satellite phone. "She would call. She always calls."

Something about the tone of his voice and the sight of the phone sends a chill down my spine. I have no physical evidence, but my psychic senses are all shouting at once.

"I've decided to help you, Jimmy, but not because I care what happened to Leticia. It's because I think people should pay for their crimes. And if something untoward happened to your boss, then whoever is at fault is going to prison." I plop down on one of the boat cushions and scowl in the hired gun's general direction. "Call me when you have a body."

My harsh words register a flicker of shock on

Jimmy's face. "That's the problem. No one's going to look for the body. I need someone—"

In an instant, I'm on my feet. "You need someone who's dating the local sheriff." My hands wave wildly in frustration. "You know, for someone who spent so many years around a master criminal, you're failing miserably at the art of subtlety."

My dad steps between us and, shockingly, his harsh words are for me. "That's enough, Mitzy. We're not here to judge people for the choices they make. You said you wanted to bring the murderer to justice—if there is one. Let's focus on that."

I scoff and roll my eyes. "Fine. What do you need me to do?"

Jimmy extends the satellite phone toward me. "Can you ask the sheriff to get some divers to the wreck?"

"No idea. I'll do my best." Snatching the phone from his hand, I call Erick.

In a flash, his all-business tone sounds over the line. "Sheriff Harper. If this is an emergency, please hang up and call 911."

"Erick, it's me."

There's a strange pause. "Mitzy? Did you get a new phone?"

"It's a long story. The punchline is there's a better-than-average chance Leticia Whitecloud was murdered and her body stashed on board her own gambling ship before it sank. I'm calling to see if you could get a couple of divers assigned to check the wreckage."

There's a slow exhale and the hint of a low whistle. "It must be a long story. Do you trust your source?"

I glare at Jimmy. "Barely."

Erick chuckles. "Good enough for me. Send me GPS coordinates for the wreck and I'll talk to the Coast Guard about divers."

The call ends abruptly and I pass the phone back to Jimmy. "He needs GPS coordinates for the wreckage."

"No problem. I activated the emergency beacon during the evacuation procedure." He taps the keys on his phone, waits for an incoming beep, and looks up. "Should I text it to the number you just called?"

"Yep."

He sends the text and the tension in his broad shoulders lessens a fraction of a percentage. He slips the phone back inside his jacket.

Jacob steps forward. "Hand over your gun, Jimmy."

The thug opens his mouth to protest, but I'm on my feet in a second. "One phone call from me, and the search is off. Hand over your gun now, or grab yourself some scuba gear."

Jimmy hangs his head, reaches into his over-the-shoulder holster, and hands me his weapon.

"And the backup piece?" I have no idea if he has one, but in the movies the bad guys always have a backup piece.

A tiny flash of admiration sparks through his eyes before he bends and retrieves the second gun from his ankle holster.

"Thanks for your cooperation."

Standing on the deck of the family yacht with a gun in each hand might be a good look for an heiress-turned-vigilante movie poster, but when I catch sight of Nimkii leading the survivors down to our boat, I panic.

My father has always been a quick study, and it only takes him a second to assess the situation. "There's a locked compartment underneath the sink in the head." He tosses me the keys and nods toward the stairs leading below deck.

There's probably a lot of military and yachtie lingo that I'm not familiar with, but I've seen enough films to know what "the head" is. Plus, if I were confused, sinks only appear in kitchens and bathrooms, so a process of elimination would eventually lead me to the secret compartment.

As I struggle with comfortably crouching in such a tiny space below deck, the thud of many pairs of feet rumble across topside.

Expecting to find the compartment empty, I freeze when I catch sight of three fat stacks of bills.

Does my dad even know these are here? Maybe grandpa Cal kept a ready supply of bribes on board in case some law enforcement official caught him with one of his illegal hunting prizes. No time to worry about that now! My father's calling for the keys.

Checking to make sure I've properly set the safety on both weapons, I place them in the compartment, re-secure it, and hurry topside.

Jacob holds one of his large hands in the air like a catcher's mitt. "Keys?"

I cautiously toss the ring. Sports are not really my thing, and I'm genuinely concerned that a full-strength throw could land the keys overboard.

My super-coordinated dad snatches them out of the air, and our boat roars to life.

Nimkii hands me a case of water, says his good-byes, and offers to let the remaining survivors stay until they clean things up on the mainland.

"Thanks. You'll let us know if anything—" I lower my voice "—or anyone, washes ashore?"

He nods once and disembarks.

Jimmy has already coiled the ropes fore and aft. Jacob eases us away from the dock.

Moving among the survivors, I introduce myself and hand out bottles of water.

"Thank you. My family and I came up from the city for the festival. Never did check the weather." Two small children clutch their father like a life raft, and the silent mother's faraway look speaks volumes.

"I'm glad you made it to shore safely."

Most of the other stories are similar, but suddenly the narrative changes.

"So, you were on the casino boat? What's your name?"

"Tripp Kenosha." The young man nods. "Yeah, it was my first gig on the boat. I bus tables in the restaurant at the casino, but they promised me a promotion if I'd work on the boat during the festival. Not the casino people. They would fire me if they knew I took a boat job. But the boat pays more, you know what I mean?"

"Sure, Tripp. More money. How many people were on board?"

He stops, looks down at his fingers, and must be reciting a silent list of names.

"Seven crew, I think. Not counting Ms. Whitecloud. We were heading to the pier to pick up passengers."

I nod my head to the side. "Does that count include Jimmy?"

He averts his gaze from the hired gun and shakes his head almost imperceptibly.

"Then there were eight?"

A wave of fear rolls off the boy as he leans toward me. "Jimmy wasn't on board."

"Are you sure? I thought he was helping people into the lifeboats?"

The young boy shrugs. "I don't see how. There weren't any lifeboats."

I hand him a bottle of water and loudly change the subject. "Let me know if you get cold. We have some blankets stowed."

Purposely avoiding Jimmy's gaze, I complete my rounds and hand out the rest of the water.

"Dad, can I talk to you below deck?"

He leans back and raises an eyebrow.

I hope the look on my face encourages him not to ask.

"Jimmy, take the wheel. We're headed back to the marina."

Jimmy nods and relieves my father.

Great. I'm not crazy about the substitute driver, but the quarters are too close to make a protest up here. I lead the way below.

Stepping into one of the cabins, I close the lacquered wooden door behind us and take a deep breath.

"What's going on, Mitzy. You look pretty worked up."

"It could just be post-traumatic stress, but the

skinny dark-haired guy up there was a crew member on the casino ship. He said Jimmy wasn't on board. And there were no lifeboats."

My dad's eyes widen as his jaw clenches tight. "Did the kid say if he saw Leticia, alive and well, once they were underway?"

"I didn't ask. He's pretty shook up, and I could tell he was worried Jimmy would overhear."

"Makes sense. I'll keep Jimmy occupied in a boisterous conversation at the helm. You question the boy about Leticia. I know Jimmy was a loyal soldier, but if Leticia put his kid in harm's way again . . . All I'm saying is, I'd hate to be on the wrong side of that guy."

"Yeah, asking me to help is the perfect way to make himself look innocent."

Jacob bites his lip. "And keep himself informed of the investigation's progress."

I nod my agreement and return to the deck.

As promised, my father starts a hilarious conversation about some of the trouble he and Jimmy got into in high school.

I grab what's left of the case of water and pretend to make another round. Standing next to the young man from the sunken gambling vessel, I continue my interrogation. "One more quick question, Tripp. Did you actually see Leticia Whitecloud walking around the ship after you were underway?"

He hugs his arms around his scrawny shoulders and chews his upper lip. "The staff had to be on board an hour before departure. Also, I think there were more than seven, because I didn't count the guy driving the boat or his sidekick."

"The captain and the first mate?" Has this kid actually never seen a *Love Boat* rerun?

"Oh, sure."

"You were saying something about Leticia." He's either majorly traumatized or he's a few cards short of a full deck.

"I was? Oh yeah, she made a pass through every deck. Mostly yelling at anyone whose uniform wasn't clean. Plus there was one guy who got fired for being drunk."

"That was before you were underway. And you never saw her after you departed from the casino?"

"Oh, we're not allowed to dock at the casino. We all had to board at the marina. We were supposed to meet Jimmy and the rest of the crew at the pier where the marks were waiting."

"Marks?"

"Yeah, that's what they call the folks who get on board to gamble."

Nodding my head. I pat him on the back and hand him another water. Slipping below, I stow the rest of the water bottles, while my father wraps up his walk down memory lane with Jimmy.

Jacob helps the passengers disembark at the marina, and Jimmy promises to check in with us later. "If you hear anything, you'll update me, right?"

I nod my head and offer a couple yep yeps. "If I don't hear from Erick in the next hour or two, I'll give him a call. The divers will have to halt the search when the sun sets."

Jimmy nods and shoves one hand in his pocket. Earlier, I wouldn't have thought anything of it. But now the nervous energy registering on my psychic radar carries a very different message.

Before we pull away from the pier, my dad jogs below deck and returns. "All clear."

"What do you mean, all clear? Did you think someone might stowaway?"

"Not exactly. But I wouldn't put it past Jimmy to stash some kind of bomb on board, if he had something to do with Leticia's death."

The assumption makes the hairs on the back of my neck stand on end. "Speaking of things stashed on board, did you know there's at least fifty grand in that locked compartment?"

The sound of my dad's hearty laughter surprises me. "That's still down there? Boy, Cal really did run this town. When I was a kid, I figured a lot of the stories of his influence were exaggerated, but, as I've taken over the business, I've learned far too many of the rumors were true."

"Are you saying grandpa Cal was not exactly on the up and up?"

"I'm saying my father was a shrewd business-man. Also, I'm sort of saying that shrewd business-men, in this country, tend to walk a fine line between legal and unlawful."

I scrunch up my lips in preparation to protest, but I'm unable to find a solid counterpoint.

We head into open water as my cell phone rings. I answer Erick's call on the first ring.

The message is not what I expected, and I catch my father's eyes.

He struggles to read the look on my face and patiently waits for me to end the call.

"Is it bad?"

"I suppose it's no worse than we expected."

CHAPTER 7

I'M NOT SURE what report I'd hoped to get from Erick. Perhaps the world would be better off without someone like Leticia Whitecloud pulling strings behind the scenes, but I can't honestly get behind wishing she were dead. "We need to head back out on the lake, Dad."

"Do we have to identify the body? Should we let Jimmy know?"

Shaking my head, I slip my phone into my pocket and sigh. "The divers didn't find anything. But I know something they don't."

He waits for me to fill him in, but grows impatient and lifts his hands. "Well?"

"She has a hidden office below deck. I found it when we were on the ship for that horrible rich woman's memorial. Do you remember? With the sniveling kids and the over-the-top gorgeous Greek widower?"

My father swallows once. "Unfortunately, I remember."

Jacob motors back toward the area where we last observed the Coast Guard vessel.

The winds have picked up and the waves are choppy, which brings an unsettling swirling to my stomach. I turn toward the bow and look straight out across the water. If I can find a steady point on the horizon, I may be able to prevent an embarrassing incident.

My observant and thoughtful dad attempts to steer into the waves and reduce the bouncing as much as possible.

"There!" My finger aims toward the cutter on the horizon.

As we approach, my father jumps on the radio to make nice with the officials. No point in causing alarm.

Lucky for us, the woman in charge of this vessel is the same one who helped us out earlier when my dad rescued the man from the capsized sailboat.

"Hey, are you good Samaritans still helping with the rescue efforts?"

Jacob smiles politely, but takes no credit. "Do you have any update on the man we pulled from the boat?"

Her wide smile says it all. "He regained consciousness en route to the ambulance at the marina and could answer questions competently. I'm sure he'll make a full recovery."

"That's great to hear. My daughter has some information that may help you with the current search operation."

I step closer to my dad and smile nervously. "Sheriff Harper tells me you're having trouble finding a body in the Hawk Island Floating Casino's wreckage."

"That's correct, miss. I brought the divers up and we're preparing to end the operation."

"Can you ask them if they found a hidden door below deck between the stateroom and the stairwell?"

Her eyes widen. "A hidden door?"

"That's right. There's a release at the top, right under the molding. It reveals a secret office that was used by the missing person."

She calls the divers aft and asks about their search.

They found no such room and weren't looking for any hidden doors.

"Best come aboard. The divers would like you to draw a map of the passageway you're describing. We have precious little daylight left. If they can proceed directly to the correct vector, it's our best chance for success."

"Copy that." I awkwardly attempt a ship-to-ship transfer, slip dangerously, and narrowly avoid winding up in the lake myself, thanks to the quick actions of my dad.

Once I've boarded the Coast Guard vessel, they provide me with paper and pencil. Closing my eyes, I psychically replay the clip of my last trek through the decks of the Hawk Island Floating Casino.

Descending the stairs, now I count my strides along the hall. I have to step into a room to avoid discovery. I attempt to pick up my count where I left off, but the math in my psychic recall is getting fuzzy. My vision gives me a clear picture of the notched molding, and it's directly across from a built-in cupboard.

"Miss, are you shipshape?"

My eyes pop open, and I stare at the captain in confusion. For a moment, I got lost in the memory and forgot where I was. "Sure. Yeah, I'm fine. I was just trying to remember as much as possible."

She nods and the divers lean in as I trace out the corridor, marking the hidden room I saw in my vision, across from the built-in cabinet, with an "X."

"That's incredibly detailed. How long ago were you on this vessel?"

That's clearly a convoluted story. It would be

foolish to tell them it was over six months ago. A time frame like that would only make them more suspicious. "Not that long ago." Before they can ask any additional questions, I carefully describe the notch that will open the hidden door.

The divers nod.

"Let the twidget know you're gonna float test this theory."

"Aye, aye." They gear up, notify their techie, and dive for a final search of the casino ship.

I offer to return to the yacht, but the friendly captain encourages me to stay on her vessel.

Under the circumstances, I'd hate to argue with her, but if those divers surface with a body, I'm outta here.

The ringing of my phone breaks the tension. "It's Sheriff Harper. Is it all right if I answer?"

A knowing smile lights up her face. "Of course. We don't want him to worry."

"Right. Thanks." Holding the phone close to my ear, I turn away in search of a sliver of privacy. "Hey, Erick."

He's worried and hopes that I'm not still out on the lake at this hour.

"Everything's fine. I'm with the Coast Guard now."

He exhales loudly.

"Don't be like that. I had some information that

was pertinent to the search and recovery mission. I'm sure the divers will be up any minute, and I'll be on my way."

The captain of the vessel grins and nods once.

"Yep, the captain just confirmed it."

He has to check in on two more temporary shelters and authorize a local family access to their home to retrieve essentials, but he wants to stop by and see me after he finishes his duties.

"Sure. That would be fine, Sheriff."

His relieved chuckle is everything right now.

The divers surface with something bobbing between them, and my heart drops to my stomach. "I've gotta go. The scuba guys are back."

Turning my eyes away from the morbid buoy, I struggle to make peace with my roiling stomach. Apparently, my insufferable mood ring picks now as the perfect time to send a message. The finger on my left hand stings with an icy stab, and I stare into the swirling black mists within the vintage gold-encircled cabochon.

A steak knife solidifies for a moment and vanishes.

I run to the side of the boat and toss my last meal overboard in an unladylike fashion. My father runs to the starboard side of his yacht and leans toward me. "Mitzy, are you seasick, or is it something else?"

I wipe the back of my hand across my mouth and take a ragged breath. "She was stabbed."

Jacob shakes his head. "Don't say anything."

"Copy that."

During my upchuck-related antics, the frogmen have hoisted their catch to the deck. The captain approaches slowly and places a firm hand on my back. "You're free to leave, Miss Moon. If you weren't a friend of Sheriff Harper's, I'm afraid I'd be taking you in. I wouldn't expect many more people than the victim and the murderer to know about a secret room below deck on the gambling ship."

Breathing a sigh of relief, I swallow and struggle to find my voice. "Understood."

She motions for me to proceed back to my vessel, but my inner snoop won't be silenced. "Was it foul play?"

The captain crosses her arms. "I suppose you've earned at least that much of the story. Victim was stabbed—in the back."

Yikes! In the back. I know Leticia wasn't short on enemies, but that seems an especially telling homicide. "Anything notable about the weapon?"

The captain shakes her head, puts a hand under my elbow, and physically lifts me across to my waiting dad. "The Coast Guard appreciates your assistance. Safe travels."

Jacob curves an arm around me and tugs a blanket across my shoulders. "Seems like she was in a hurry to get you off her ship."

Collapsing onto one of the oilcloth boat cushions, I tug the warm blanket tightly around me. "You'll never guess what happened. I asked one too many questions."

He chuckles heartily, starts the engines, and heads toward the marina.

The world has one less villain, and I have one more mystery. Regardless of the fact that Jimmy is currently my primary suspect, I promised to help him.

Time to give him a quick, vague update. I keep it short and sweet. No details about my vision or my suspicions. Just a body was recovered. Coast Guard will hand it over to the medical examiner.

There's nothing more to be done today. The beautiful pinkish-orange sunset shows no trace of the day's catastrophes. What I need right now is a long, hot shower, a delicious, comfort-food snack, and the strong arms of the sexy sheriff.

The sketchy drive back to my bookshop is all a blur to me. Jacob handles everything expertly and promises to board up my windows in the morning.

I'm sure I answered him, although I don't remember words coming out of my mouth.

Stumbling through the heavy metal door from the alley, I still have the blanket from the yacht wrapped around my shoulders.

Letting it drop on the floor, I toy with the idea of unhooking the "No Admittance" chain across the bottom of the wrought-iron circular staircase. But in my current state, I can't remember the code to shut off the alarm. The little chunk of my common sense that is still ticking knows that Twiggy rigged the alarm to a back-up power system.

I leave it hooked, tempt fate, and climb over the chain. I catch my toe and teeter precariously on the step.

"Reeeee-ow." A warning.

The shocking sound from the bottom of the staircase causes me to lurch forward. I grab the handrail and steady myself. The excitement of seeing Pyewacket up and around drowns any harsh words he may deserve. "What's up, son? You look about a thousand percent better."

"Reow." Can confirm.

"Why don't you go warm up a spot for me in that big cozy bed? I need a steaming shower and then I'll be getting off my feet for the rest of the night."

Without responding, Pyewacket elegantly

bounds up the stairs with grace and power. He paces next to the open secret door as I trudge across the loft.

Now, to hustle upstairs and answer the call of the shower—

Ghost-ma senses my return and is over-excited, as usual. "Mitzy! You're finally back, and you're safe!"

"I wish I could say the same for Leticia Whitecloud."

"Oh dear! Is she dead?"

"Stabbed in the back by someone. We'll set up the murder board in the morning."

The spirit in the amulet groans, and my own heart pinches with sadness. In the good old days, before the cursed jewelry trapped my grandmother, she used to write out the 3 x 5 cards for me while I pinned them to the rolling corkboard supplied by Twiggy. We always worked together to connect suspects with the victim using green yarn, because the red yarn scared my resident ghost.

"I miss the good old days, sweetie."

"Me too. But you like being able to go to the diner with me, now."

"Boy, do I. That Odell Johnson is a fine man. I'll always regret divorcing him, but I'm thankful he found it in his heart to spend my last months with me, allowing me to make it up to him."

It occurs to me that I should conserve my cell phone battery. "Do we have candles?"

"In that drawer where we keep the pendulum. There should be a box of candles and several holders."

I pop open the drawer and light one candle. Then it's time for phone off and operation Olden Times to begin.

Placing two candles on the coffee table, one at the bedside and one in the bathroom, I nod. "That should do nicely." A hint of the match's smoke drifts through the air, leaving a tinge of sulfur.

"RE-OW!" Game on!

My head whip pans to the beast. "Oh, no you don't! We've already had wind and water disasters today. Don't you dare race around here, knock over a candle, and start a fire!"

His large, golden eyes sparkle in the candle-light, but I hope we have an accord.

Halfway to the bathroom, my socks and shoes off and the hem of my fancy red shirt around my ears, my grandmother's comment about Odell pops into my head. "I know you were pretty sick, at the end, but when you say 'make it up to him.' What does that mean?" I snicker involuntarily.

She gasps. "Well, I never!"

Laughing as I continue my path toward the shower, I shout a familiar refrain. "Oh, Myrtle

Isadora Johnson Linder Duncan Willamet Rogers, we both know that's not true!"

Her heartwarming laughter follows me into the next room.

The glorious hot water, luxurious steam, and rejuvenating eucalyptus bath products envelop me. The days of struggling under an intermittent stream of ice-cold water are behind me. Even after all these months, I still appreciate every second of toasty warm water cascading over my body.

"That was amazing!"

Grams scoffs. "I hope you enjoyed it! That was likely a third of the hot water left in the boiler. If they don't get the power restored by tomorrow, you'll be back to cold showers in no time."

"Can't I get a generator?"

"*After* a storm?" Her voice is thick with shock and sarcasm. "Any generator that survived the twister has been snapped up. You're looking at pioneer living until the city gets this all sorted out."

Shrugging my shoulders, I finish drying my hair with the thick cotton towel and drop it on the floor.

Pye raises his head and seems to scowl.

"I'll pick it up later. I promise. Now, make room. After a quick rest and recuperate, I'll set up the murder thingy."

My fiendish feline doesn't budge.

An oddity in the bowls beside the bed grabs my

attention. "You didn't finish your Fruity Puffs. You left three. I'm sure a big boy like you has room for three little puffs."

He curls tightly and lets his tail cover his eyes.

"Too tired to argue. Make way."

He remains motionless and makes neither a way nor anything else. I curl around him and close my eyes for a minute, regardless of the lack of invitation.

CHAPTER 8

BANG. BANG. BANG.

What is that infernal pounding—

My eyelids fly up like misbehaving roller shades. "Erick!" I leap out of bed, trip over the towel I left on the floor, and spiral in time to land firmly on my ample backside. "Shoot! Shoot! Shoot! I look like warmed-over death."

A quick check in the mirror confirms my worst fears. I fell asleep with wet hair and it dried in all kinds of horrible ways.

Grams calls out from the pendant on the bed. "At least you're clean."

"Hush! I'm hanging you in the closet. I expect you to mind your manners, or I'll relocate you to the printing museum. Understood?"

"Aye, aye, Captain."

I can almost see her diamond-adorned hand popping a sarcastic salute. Grabbing the necklace from the bed, I rush into the closet, hang her on a hook, and pull the door closed with a loud click.

She mumbles some snarky quip, but I'm already through my permanently open—at least until power is restored—bookcase door and picking my way down the staircase.

After my recent spill next to the four-poster bed, I take my time climbing over the chain and walk cautiously to the side door. Opening it slowly, I paste on a huge smile, which I hope will distract from the white haystack on top of my head.

The halogen glow of a flashlight illuminates Erick's amused grin and proves my efforts are in vain. "Gosh, Moon. No need to get all dolled up on my account."

My shoulders droop and I slouch forward in defeat. "Seriously, I tried. Hey, I took a shower." I point to my clean person and my cute shorty pajamas.

He takes his time dragging the beam of his torch from my head to my toes and back again, and nods. "Go on."

A flush of heat flashes across my skin. "Listen, I didn't mean to fall asleep. But you should be honored. I showered before I had anything to eat."

A triumphant grin spreads across his face, and I'm unsure whether I've won or lost.

He pulls his hand from behind his back and offers me the to-go bag in his grip.

The unmistakably delicious aroma reveals the contents before I open the sack. "Fries! Has anyone told you today that you're the best boyfriend ever?"

He releases the bag to my grasp and rubs a thumb along his stubbled chin. "Well, you're only telling me this right now, so if someone else had told me earlier, wouldn't that be of concern to you?" His laughter erupts before I can answer his diabolical question.

"All right, smart guy. I suppose I'm the only one who gets to call you 'boyfriend.' I get it. You don't have to take everything so literally."

He rolls back on his heels. "Are you going to invite me in, or do I need a warrant?"

The idea of him searching me brings little goosebumps to my forearms. "Come in. Come in. Sorry, I'm barely awake."

Leading the way upstairs with the help of his light, I force myself to remain calm as he shares an update.

"I spoke to the Coast Guard, and they've turned the body over to the medical examiner. There were sixteen fatalities today, but fortunately only one was murder. The rest can be attributed to the superstorm. Not even the top meteorologists predicted the destruction that hit Pin Cherry. There'll be a community-wide memorial service next weekend. They've rescheduled the Midsummer Bonfire in honor of those we lost."

His voice cracks, and my heart aches for him. I know he lost too many friends in Afghanistan, and losing civilian lives hits him hard. Maybe I can lift his spirits by shifting the focus to the loss of life that can't be blamed on the storm. "When can we get our hands on the ME's report on Leticia?"

He kicks off his shoes, plunks down on the sofa, and pulls me onto his lap. "I know how you get when you're on a case, but if we could talk about anything besides death for a couple of hours, I'm sure I can make it worth your while." His finger traces the neckline of my pajama top.

And . . . I'm dead. This man has a way with words, and other stuff. "If you'll allow me a few french fries, I can bring you up to speed on Stellen's orientation week and my foundation's plans to assist in rebuilding the library."

He leans back, pulls my feet onto his lap, and gently massages the stress away while I make small talk and munch on potato perfection.

Candles shrink as time slips away, and, if not for the thievery of precious fries by my wildcat, I may have drifted off to sleep again myself.

"Pyewacket! You furry fiend!"

Erick rouses from his extreme relaxation, slides my feet to the floor, and stands. "I better head home and get some sleep." He yawns and stretches his arms high in the air.

Yes! I get a peek at his abs. Yes, he catches me in the act and grins.

"Can't say I'm sorry my mother picked this week to visit her sister in Chicago. It would've been difficult to focus on rescue efforts if she were in danger."

In case you missed a memo, Erick bought his mom a house in Pin Cherry when he returned from Afghanistan. Her eyesight is failing, so he lives with her and helps her out. It's terribly sweet, but does put a dampener on our dating situation. "Guess I'll see you tomorrow?"

He sighs heavily, but a wistful smile turns up the corners of his mouth. "I'll text you when I hear from the ME, and maybe we can peruse the report over lunch. I asked her to prioritize the Coast Guard's case over the other— Well, you know."

Nodding immediately, I refuse to repeat the victim's name or anything about the additional casualties. "Makes sense." Purposely standing between him and his shoes, I slip my hands around his neck. "You can stay, you know."

A flicker of mischief flashes through his beautiful blue eyes as he slides his hands around my waist. "Offer accepted."

Grasping his hand, I try to lead him toward my bed.

"Hold on." He tugs me back a pace or two and bends to blow out the candles. "Safety first."

For some reason, that gives me a case of the giggles. However, I get myself under control and proceed toward the bedside candle. I swear there's a chuckle and a "woot" as I pass the closet. I'll ignore it. I can be the better person.

My wise old caracal abandons ship as we approach the bed. I'm sure he'll slip outside during the night, through one of his secret exits, despite my request that he stay indoors until he's fully healed.

The lack of power is forgotten, as a different kind of electricity sparks in the candlelight.

Soft lips press against mine, and the only thing I'm sure of is that morning will come too soon.

The distraction of my coed sleepover caused forgetful little me to leave the blackout shades undeployed. The stark lemon-yellow light of an early summer morning pierces my eyelids.

My first instinct is to groan, roll over, and pull the comforter over my head.

Then I remember my guest.

Cracking one eyelid open, I drink in the curve of his ear, the fullness of his lips, and that—

SNORT. Cough. Gasp.

"Erick Harper! You snore!"

He rubs his eyes, and a moment later the bright-blue pools engulf me. "At least I don't talk in my sleep."

Blerg. Busted. "Did I say anything incriminating?"

Snickering, he pulls me close. "Sometimes I wonder if it would be possible for you to say anything that wasn't incriminating. There was some mumbling about a secret room, something about up-chucking, and at least one reference to someone named Ben? Should I be worried?"

"Oh brother." I pull the comforter over my head and softly scream. From underneath my embarrassment shield, I toss out a weak defense. "It was probably all about the Coast Guard search. Leticia had a hidden room below deck. I found it when I attended that memorial thing last year. It's not something divers would look for, so that's what I was doing with the Coast Guard. Of course, when they brought up the—don't make me say it—I got a little sick over the side."

He gently tugs the cover from my face and traces his finger down my nose and over my lips.

"That explains two-thirds. Care to try your hand at the bit about Shady Ben?"

My eyes roll, and I can feel my cheeks hot with color. "I don't think we're at that place where we swap stories about our exes, are we?"

Somehow I chose the right phrase, because he instantly drops the subject and leans away. However, that only serves to make me curious. I roll over and rest my chin on his broad chest. "You gave up way too easy, Sheriff. Maybe we do need to swap stories about the past."

He silences me with a kiss and quickly rolls out of bed. "I have time for breakfast, but only barely. How fast can you get ready?"

"Offer accepted. I can be ready in five."

He nods and hits the stopwatch on his phone.

"You've got to be flipping kidding me!" I race to the closet to put yesterday's tee on instant replay and have to endure locker-room taunts from my invasive grandmother. I send her a quick thought threat. *You'll pay for your insolence.*

Her chuckles make me smile, and I hustle into the bathroom to splash some water on my face and hair.

When I emerge from the bathroom dressed and only dripping a little, Erick hits stop. "Four minutes, forty-two seconds. That's a new record, Moon. I think you've earned yourself half of a caramel sticky bun."

"You know me so well."

Of course, he's completely dressed and looks absolutely perfect. This isn't the first time we've had breakfast together at the diner, but it's the first time we had breakfast together after spending the *night* together. I feel like everyone will know.

CHAPTER 9

As I PUSH open the thick wooden door at the front of my bookshop, we're greeted by the incessant beeping of heavy machinery backing up.

Erick offers a friendly wave, and the bulldozer comes to a stop.

The former snowplow driver, Artie, jumps out of the cab and strides toward us. "Mornin', Sheriff. Mornin', Mitzy." Her curly grey-brown hair pokes out from under a baseball cap, and a lightweight plaid cotton shirt hangs over a plain white tee.

My boyfriend seems to handle this "tryst discovery" incident with no embarrassment, so I struggle to follow suit. "Good morning, Artie. Now I see how the city keeps you busy during the off-season."

She grins, nods, and juts a thumb toward the

bulldozer. "With the amount of rubble I need to clear from the streets, I'll be driving this thing twenty-four-hours a day for the next week."

Erick shakes his head. "That's no good. I have calls out to Broken Rock and a couple other municipalities. We should have additional dozers helping with cleanup efforts by this afternoon."

She bobs her head appreciatively. "Not that I mind the overtime during our three months of poor sledding weather, Sheriff, but I could sure use the help. The utility repair guys won't be able to get through until I clear 'em a path. That's where I'm focusing my efforts, but between you and me, citizens feel better when the roads are clear. They'll be all right without power for a day or two. Folks around here are always prepared. But seeing the roads full of debris, that's what they find disheartening."

He smiles. "I agree. You clear the way for the power company, and I'll make sure backup arrives sooner, rather than later."

She swats him hard on the shoulder and smiles. "That right there is why they keep reelecting you. You really do care about the people in this county." Artie climbs back into the bulldozer with the spry movements of a woman half her age, raises her thermos of coffee in a toast, and shouts, "Still love the shirt, Mitzy."

Blerg. That's what I get for rehashing my wardrobe.

We continue picking our way down the block toward the diner.

Erick opens the door for me, and I take a sustaining breath before walking through to the black-and-white checkerboard of linoleum.

The diner is wall-to-wall with customers. All eyes, and I mean every last set, turn toward us with a mélange of surprise, amusement, mild shock, and maybe even a fleck or two of jealousy.

Odell offers a spatula salute from the kitchen and waves us over. "I've got a card table and chairs set up in the alley. You're welcome to have a seat out there away from the looky-loos, and I'll have your food up faster than you can say Peter Piper picked a peck of pickled peppers."

The unexpected tongue twister sends me into a fit of giggles, and Erick scoops an arm around my waist as he leads me through the kitchen to the private table.

The thrumming of the generator is anything but soothing. However, I'd choose it over prying eyes any day of the week.

Tally's daughter brings our coffee, smirks and gives me a wink.

Erick pretends not to notice any of it. "Good

thing you're home for the summer. Your mom can definitely use the help today."

Tatum rolls her eyes. "Yeah, lucky me. Home for the worst tornado in Pin Cherry's history." She laughs and shrugs. "Any of the cit-iots that could hightailed it out of town yesterday. But there are still a heckuva lot of folks whose cars are blocked by downed trees, or, worse, crushed under them. So we've been feeding folks in shifts since six o'clock this morning."

Sheriff Harper reaches up and pats her shoulder. "Thanks for helping out. We're all doing what we can."

She bites her lip to keep from smirking and flashes her eyebrows at me as she leaves.

Sadly, Erick feels the embarrassed flush on my cheeks must be addressed. "How you doing over there, Moon?" He lifts his chin.

"I feel a little like a front-page story in a trashy gossip rag, but other than that . . . Splendid."

He laughs and exhales. "You know how it is in a small town. No business is your own business. I'm proud to call you my girlfriend, and I don't care who knows it."

The color in my cheeks doubles down as Odell bangs through the screen door with our breakfast.

"You two sure are doing your part."

"What do you mean?"

The creases around his eyes deepen as he stifles a chuckle. "Folks need something to take their mind off the aftermath of the superstorm. There's nothing like hot gossip to do the trick." He raps his knuckles twice on the flimsy card table and disappears into the kitchen, chuckling all the way.

Erick shoves a huge bite of blueberry pancakes into his mouth and grins stupidly.

Taking a sip of coffee, I attempt to process my current situation. "I suppose I can look at all of this as one giant selfless gesture for my community."

He grabs a napkin and covers his mouth. For a moment he chokes on his giant mouthful of breakfast-y goodness, but eventually manages to wash it down with a gulp of coffee. "Careful, Moon. We can't have the sheriff choking to death in the middle of a crisis." Wiping his chin with the flimsy paper, he sighs. "I'm sure I'll be running and gunning until well after dark. You want me to check in on you later?"

"I would very much like a check-in, Sheriff."

"Consider it done." He shoves another forkful of syrupy flapjacks into his mouth and nods.

Tingly happiness bounces through my body as I inhale the welcome aromas and dive into my amazing breakfast.

We part company with a lengthy kiss in the alley. He heads off to the station, and I duck inside for a refill of liquid alert.

I chew the fat with Odell while sipping glorious black gold.

"Looks like you've got a visitor." He nods toward the front door.

Glancing over my shoulder, I instantly recognize the purposeful shuffle of my attorney and alchemist, Silas Willoughby.

"You're back!" Without a care for propriety, I slip my empty mug into the bus bin behind the counter, weave through the crowded tables, and hug my mentor tightly.

"That's quite enough, Mizithra." He harrumphs into his bushy grey mustache.

"Sorry, I'm so happy to see you! I lost all sense of decorum."

This excuse brings a brief chuckle. "Oh, is that the reason *du jour*?"

"Rude." He smiles and I inform him of the special table out back.

He follows without hesitation, and I agree to another cup of coffee from Tatum, while he enjoys his breakfast. "Seems like everyone's already talking about how I'm helping with the library situation."

He nods his head and his jowls waggle. "That's the way of things here. We'll survey the site today, and I'll put a proposal together for the city's approval." Silas carefully consumes his egg-white omelet, wipes his magnificent mustache, and pushes back from the temporary seating. "Is there an update on Pyewacket?"

"Geez! I can't believe it wasn't the first thing out of my mouth. My dad found him, cleaned up his cut, and the spoiled feline is as good as new."

"Ah, that is a deep relief."

"For reals. I'll take care of your dishes. I'm assuming we're walking over to—disaster central. Is that what we're calling it?" Scooping up his place setting, I head toward the back door.

"Thank you. And I'm certain the storm's destruction will come to be known by many names. Not the least of which will be disaster. We shall indeed make the best progress on foot."

Shop owners and helpful neighbors are busy with cleanup efforts. Perhaps the storm wasn't as epic as the rumors make it sound. Many of the shops along Main Street and Third Avenue are intact.

It's not until we reach the patisserie that the tornado's true power becomes clear.

The owner of Bless Choux is filling a wheelbarrow with broken glass, smashed pastries, and other debris.

"Morning, Anne. Is most of your damage superficial? This looks like a lot of glass."

She leans on her shovel and sighs with relief. "If we were one block this way, the whole place would be gone. That's the thing about tornadoes. They slice right through a community, obliterating houses on one side of the street, and leaving the others untouched. This may be a sorry sight, but most of it is fallout from the debris cloud."

"I'm glad the bakery is going to be all right. Do you need help with cleanup?"

She shakes her head and points over her shoulder, through the broken front window, into the shop. "My husband called his brothers up from Grand Falls last night. They arrived with the sun this morning, and they're putting everything right. They brought me a generator, so we should be able to reopen tomorrow. Of course, the windows will be boarded up for a while. But I'll let the glaziers help the folks that are in real trouble before I worry about getting a simple window replaced."

"It's good you have help. You let me know if there's anything the foundation can do, won't you?"

She smiles and wipes a ready tear from the corner of her eye. "Thank you. But if you're taking on the library project, I think that's enough goodwill for this community. That beautiful building was dead center of the twister's path. Strange funnel cloud, if you ask me. Not real wide, but they say when the storm draws its arms in like a figure skater, that's when it really spins."

"Oh, wow." The more I learn about these tornadoes, the more I hope I never experience another. "I'll see you later this week for a chocolate croissant. Deal?"

She nods and wipes a trickle of sweat from her brow, leaving a dirty streak. "Deal."

Walking into the swath of destruction left by the tornado takes my breath away. A block away, City Hall stands firm, with nothing more than broken windowpanes and two downed trees.

On our side of the street, where the historic library once stood, there is nothing but the memory of a once beautiful building. The remains remind me of the partially standing castle ruins I've read about littering the hills in Ireland.

Silas pauses, removes a handkerchief from his pocket, and dabs at his eyes. "Some of these books are irreplaceable."

"We'll do everything we can to restore the collection, Silas. With my money, your ingenuity, and Twiggy's contacts—"

He solemnly nods his agreement. "You are correct. No time to despair. This community needs a cause to rally around. The rebuilding of the library shall be a monument to Pin Cherry Harbor's resilience, and a remembrance of those who lost their lives in the storm."

My heart hurts for a moment, but the sudden flashback to the rescue divers bobbing to the surface turns my stomach in an entirely different direction. "Did I tell you Leticia Whitecloud was murdered?"

Silas crinkles up his bulbous nose and his forehead creases with concern. "You did not. I can't say I view it as a tragedy, but when did this occur?"

I fill him in on the sketchy details, and my suspicion of Jimmy's part in the unfortunate events.

"The possibility is genuine enough. Your father is correct in assuming Jimmy would not let his son return to prison for another of Ms. Whitecloud's crimes. I wouldn't rule him out if I were you."

"What's the news on Ghost-ma's situation?"

He turns toward me and smooths his mustache with thumb and forefinger. "One could suffer whiplash keeping up with your topic changes."

"Touché."

He slowly draws a ragged breath through his yellowed teeth and gazes over the rubble. "This seems an untoward location to discuss Isadora's predicament. Perhaps we may retire to the bookshop?"

"Oh, sure. Follow me."

Activity increases as the morning drags on, and

the line waiting for service at the diner wraps halfway down the block.

Silas and I wave and exchange pleasantries as we pass familiar faces waiting for Odell's delicious creations. We learn that the Piggly Wiggly has a generator and is open for cash business, and that power has already been restored to the Regional Medical Center and the animal hospital.

It surprises me to hear that the wealthy neighborhood known as "The Pines" is still without power, but I suppose tragedy is the true equalizer.

Twiggy and my father are working together to place protective boards over the cracked panels of glass.

"Hey, guys, Silas and I were going to discuss—"

He places a firm hand on my arm. "Careful. Your grandmother's situation is not for public broadcast."

I mentally slap myself on the forehead. Right. Me and my big mouth. I'll try this again. "You guys need any help?"

They take one look at me, exchange an unreadable look, and shake their heads simultaneously. Apparently no one is interested in putting me up a ladder.

"Suit yourselves. We'll be in the apartment."

They nod, and we move indoors.

Pyewacket is beside himself when he catches

sight of Silas in the scalloped-back chair. The usually aloof feline dives onto the alchemist's lap and licks his face so hard, one side of Silas's mustache twists up like that of a silent-movie villain!

"You've never been that happy to see me, Pyewacket."

Pyewacket's entire focus is on Silas. He doesn't have the bandwidth for a snarky growl.

A muffled voice in the distance catches my attention. "Whoops! Coming, Grams." I push open the door to the closet, offer a stream of apologies, and grab the pendant off the hook.

"What did Silas find out? Can he break me out of here?"

"Easy, *Escape from Alcatraz*." Dangling the amulet in one hand, I walk toward Silas. "In case you didn't guess, Grams wants to know if you're going to get her out of the pendant."

"Despite the joy of this reunion, I must turn our attention to more serious matters." Silas gestures toward the sofa. "Please sit down, Mitzy. Place your grandmother on the coffee table and share her questions with me. Now that she's trapped in that amber keep, I can't see her spirit. At least when she was free floating, her pantomime would give me some indication. Perhaps I'll deduce a way to hear her voice at some point."

Grams exhales loudly. "Tell him I don't give

two hoots about him being able to hear me! I want out of this prison!"

I take my job as an afterlife interpreter quite seriously. However, I have no intention of agitating my mentor. "Grams is eager to hear what you've discovered."

She sighs. "Good save, sweetie."

Silas laces his fingers together and rests his hands on his round paunch. "My brother and I examined *Loca Sine Lumine, Loca Sine Lege* passage by passage. He offered compelling alternate translations to my initial thoughts on the lawless paths through darkness. We endeavored to connect the themes woven through the convoluted text. Those notes, along with the information I could glean from other tomes, left me with a greater degree of certainty than I possessed prior to my trip east."

Grams makes fake snoring sounds and yawns loudly. "Tell him to cut to the chase, Mitzy. Every minute in here is like a decade!"

"Silas, I know context is important to you, but Grams gets a little dramatic."

He glances down at the pendant. "I'm sure you wish to make a hasty exit, Isadora. However, my news is not one of simple blacks and whites. This is a swirling grey tableau, which warrants a carefully considered decision. I must insist that both of you listen patiently to what I have uncovered."

Ghost-ma clicks her tongue and sniffles. "This doesn't sound good, dear. I can't lose you. But I'm not sure I can stay in here, either."

"It's all right, Grams. If it comes down to choosing between staying in the necklace to be with me or leaving the necklace and crossing over, I think it's better if you're free. I wish you could stay with me forever, but I can't keep you prisoner like some rare species in a creepy collection."

Now we're both crying, and Silas is nervously smoothing his mustache. "I must insist that the two of you cease your prattling. I have important information to share and you need to consider it in its entirety before you formulate your decision."

Grams snuffles loudly. "Tell him I promise to behave. No more interruptions. I swear."

"We're ready. Tell us everything."

"There are two forces that come into play. The pendant itself is not purposely cursed. It simply creates a wall through which a trapped spirit cannot penetrate."

"Tell me something I don't know!" Grams sighs heavily.

It's best if I don't share her snark with the alchemist.

"The second piece that must be considered is the original workings which tethered your grandmother to this bookshop. When she was placed in the amber, the tether created by my earlier efforts was broken. Jedediah and I examined the specifics of the language from many angles. The clearest truths we discovered are that the destruction of the pendant's power will ultimately free the trapped soul. However, with my tether having previously been obliterated, the freed spirit will, in all likelihood, crossover. The barriers of unfinished business have been addressed. Your grandmother's dying wish was to meet you and have a relationship with you. That occurred prior to her entrapment. We must assume that if she is released from the stone, she will leave us."

Silent tears trickle down my cheeks, and Pyewacket lays a paw over his head as though he can't bear to hear any more.

Silas steeples his fingers and bounces his chin on his pointers.

I recognize the possibilities behind that pose. A spark of hope warms my chest. There is a lesson brewing, perhaps a crazy solution.

"There is one piece of the puzzle which we were unable to accurately measure."

I lean forward eagerly. "What? Grams and I will do anything. What's the piece?"

"Your love for your grandmother could tip the scales."

My mouth goes dry and I can't swallow. My

voice comes out in a squeak. "What are you saying?"

"It is my belief that there exists a link between you and Isadora that we do not understand. Something in this plane that ties you to her. If we can enhance the power of this bond, I may be able to use that energy to recreate the broken tether. Although, to be fair, my original workings were done when Isadora was in the flesh. I have no experience transmuting the essence of a spirit."

My skin is cold and I swear I can't feel my heart beating. I'm not sure which part shocks me more, the thought of my love being the key to keeping my grandmother, or the idea that there's something Silas hasn't experienced! "What's the thing that bonds us? What if my love isn't enough? What happens to me if I mess up?"

My grandmother is oddly quiet.

Silas motions with his hands for me to simmer down. "As I said, there are a multitude of variables. You and your grandmother must carefully consider all that lies before us. Failure looms in equal measure to success."

Leaning into the soft cushions of the sofa, my heart sinks. "What do you want to do, Grams?"

Silence.

"Grams? What's wrong?"

"I need some time to think, dear. Can you put

me in the closet while you work on the murder wall? I need to be alone."

The pain in her voice breaks my heart, but the least I can do is comply with her request. "No problem. I'll leave the door open so I can hear you when—"

Her sobs are audible, and I wish there was some way I could shove an afterlife handkerchief into the pendant. "Don't worry. If love is the answer, we'll figure it out. I love you."

She chokes out her reply through her tears. "I love you too, dear."

CHAPTER 10

SILAS OFFERS TO TEMPORARILY FILL GRAMS'
role as my assistant. I wheel the corkboard to the
middle of the room and sigh loudly. Handing the
alchemist a stack of 3 x 5 cards and a pen, I pace in
front of the board and list off names.

"Pardon me, Mitzy. Is there a purpose to this
recitation of given names?"

My mouth lolls open as I turn toward him.
"What?"

He smooths his mustache with a thumb and
forefinger. "This list of names, does it have a
purpose?"

Glancing at the undisturbed stack of cards in
his lap, I roll my eyes and groan. "Right, I forgot you
were a noob."

He strokes his chin and taps it with two fingers.

"If memory serves, that term refers to an individual lacking experience in a particular field. Please elaborate."

Walking toward him, I bend and click the pen. "I say the names and you write each one on a separate card. I hate to say it, Silas, but it's so simple a ghost can literally do it."

He chuckles. "Ah. I understand. These cards are then placed on the board, and you deduce the guilt or innocence of your potential suspects. It is a visual mind map. This is quite a useful tool."

Does he think I invented this thing? His lack of pop-culture references astounds. The man possesses libraries' worth of arcane knowledge, but has he actually never seen a single crime drama? "That's the basic idea. I'll start again. Jimmy, Jimmy's son—"

"Do you mean James?"

"What now? No. He goes by Jimmy. This board is only for me, Silas. We don't need to use formal names."

"Of course. I have written the bodyguard's name on one of your little cards. However, it is my understanding that his son prefers the moniker James."

"Oh, sure. *That* you know. Let's go with James for the son then."

"Please, continue."

"My pleasure. Let's add a card with question marks, indicating someone we haven't discovered yet from the Tribal Council. Maybe add another card for Tripp Kenosha, the busboy/server from the floating casino." I toss my hands in the air in exasperation. "I don't know, Silas. Leticia had so many enemies I can't imagine where to begin."

He leans forward, placing the stack of cards and the pen meticulously on the table. "Perhaps a visit to the land-based Hawk Island Casino would assist your investigation."

"It couldn't hurt. Do you think I should call Jimmy to set it up?"

"Indeed. If he is guilty, as you suspect, it is likely that he would be of great assistance in helping you pursue any avenue that leads away from him."

"Accurate."

Checking my recent calls, I tap an unfamiliar number, place it on speaker, and hope for the best.

"Mitzy? You got an update?"

"Not since the last one, Jimmy. Still waiting for the medical examiner's report."

A low grumble of acknowledgment is his only response.

"I need to talk to some people out at the casino. Can you set that up?"

"I don't know. Maybe. Do you know if they found August Burwell?"

"Who?"

"He was Leticia's new business partner. And—I suppose you'll find out anyway—they were involved —personally."

My eyes roll dangerously, and I shake my head at Silas. I can't believe this guy! This is information that would've been super helpful, yesterday. "Why am I just hearing about this now, Jimmy? This August Burwell should be one of our prime suspects. Where was he last seen?"

"He was on the boat, with Leticia. You know, the floating casino."

I'd love to tell him the reason I don't know is that he purposely didn't tell me. I'd also like to yell about how eyewitness testimony claims Jimmy wasn't on the boat! However, I need to play my cards close to the vest until I get more information. "I'll make some calls and see if he was among the survivors. Can you get me into the casino or not?"

"I know a guy who knows a guy. Give me an hour."

"Copy that." I end the call and lift my hands in confusion.

Silas remained quiet during the call, but he confidently offers his opinion now. "I believe your instinct concerning Jimmy's concealment of facts is quite accurate. It is most disconcerting that he waylaid this information about Leticia's relationship with August Burwell. What psychic data did you gather?"

"None. It annoyed me how he lied to me, and then I was distracted by the rage."

Silas steeples his fingers, but before he can begin bouncing his chin, I jump to my defense. "Fine. I'll take a deep breath and do whatever. Give me a minute."

Sulking toward the settee and plunking down with an exasperated sigh, I crack my neck to one side and then the other. Three deep breaths. Eyes closed. I replay the call with Jimmy. He's nervous. He's absolutely hiding something. The energy around August Burwell's name is thick with mixed messages. That lead definitely needs to be pursued. I open my eyes and smile at Silas. "You were right. You are always right. We need to make a card for August Burwell."

Silas nods graciously and writes out a 3 x 5 card without so much as a smirk of "I told you so."

Pinning the cards onto the board with tacks, I run string from each suspect to the victim. An interesting bit of geometry emerges. There is a clear triangle between Jimmy, August, and Leticia. As unlikely as it seems, there's a possibility of something more than a business relationship between Jimmy and Leticia. Taking a card from the stack, I slip the pen from Silas's hand and write "love triangle?" on a blank one. I tack that in the middle of the green yarn shape. "Love or money, right?"

He nods emphatically. "Almost without exception."

Jimmy calls back sooner than expected and informs me that his connection said the current owners of the Hawk Island Casino are willing to meet with me this afternoon, but I didn't hear it from him.

Has he watched one too many gangster movies? Seems like a lot of unnecessary subterfuge.

Maybe I can distract Grams from her troubles by asking her to pick out an outfit for my meeting.

Before I can test my theory, my phone pings with a text from Erick. "Bummer. Erick has to cancel lunch, but he summarized the ME's findings. Not a huge surprise. He says Leticia died of the stab wound, which bisected the descending aorta. They have identified the weapon as a standard steak knife. There were an ample number on board as part of the ship's standard cutlery set. Anyone would've had access. No prints were recovered."

Silas leans back and inhales sharply. "That hardly assists you in your search."

"I know, right?" Getting to my feet, I write a quick "steak knife/open access" card, and drop the pen on the coffee table. "I'm going to let all of this simmer around in the old grape, while Grams picks out an outfit for me. Do you want to come with me to this meeting?"

Silas rises, adjusts his rumpled coat, and shakes his head. "I shall return to my abode and assemble my supplies. You and Isadora can handle wardrobe, and you are capable of taking this meeting unescorted. Once you and your grandmother have had the opportunity to make a decision regarding the amulet, please update me."

"All right, I guess."

He offers a brief bow of his head and takes his leave.

Pasting on a fake smile, I breeze into the closet with my news. "Grams, I have a meeting out at the casino. Can you help me find something appropriate to wear?"

No response.

"I suppose I could wear these jean culottes and this bright-yellow prairie blouse. Maybe with riding boots?"

"Goodness gracious! I would've thought you'd have learned something from me at this point!"

Bingo. Yahtzee.

She scoffs. "Oh, you think you're quite a clever girl. Never mind. Let's get busy on an appropriate outfit. You're a wealthy heiress, with powerful political connections, and you're set to single-handedly apprehend the murderer of a notorious local crime boss."

In my mind, one of her perfectly drawn eyebrows is arched, and she's biting the edge of her coral-stained lip as she taps a strand of her pearls.

"Mitzy! You really are a psychic. That's exactly what I'm doing."

We share a giggle, and I hope that I've lightened her burden for a moment.

"Let's go summer power suit, with an outrageous hat and those diamond-encrusted designer sunglasses."

Oh brother. I'm sorry I asked for her help.

"Have a little gratitude, dear. If you had to pay for it, you could never afford a stylist like me."

"Maybe not, but I also wouldn't have to continue to tell said stylist to get out of my head!"

"Sorry, sweetie. It's so easy to lose track."

"Is it though?"

She snickers. "The suit is at the far end on the left. It's a beautiful shade of summer green, and the eyelet camisole should be hanging right next to it. Let me see you in that before I decide on a hat."

Four wardrobe changes later, I wind up in a hand-dyed linen suit, with a pale-pink silk tank peeking out from under the no-lapel jacket.

"Oh, Mitzy! You look gorgeous. Let's try the

Hampton straw hat with the floppy brim. The one with the beautiful cream satin ribbon."

I push the hat on, droop my shoulders, and frown.

"Stand up straight. Angle the hat so the brim flops over one eye and grab those tortoiseshell Gucci shades from the top drawer."

Opening one of the built-in accessory drawers, I search for the sunglasses she mentioned. When I catch sight of the gun—

"Don't you dare take that weapon! You're going in there as a monied businesswoman. There's no reason to assume things will go south. Taking a gun only invites trouble."

"Perhaps, but if something goes wrong, I'd rather be the one inviting trouble than the one late to the party."

Ignoring her warning, I pick up the Springfield EMP, make sure it's loaded, double-check the safety, and place it in the straw handbag I've been instructed to pair with the outfit.

"Wish me luck!"

"You won't need luck. This is a simple fact-finding mission."

"Are you going to wish me luck, Pye?"

"Ree-ow." Soft but condescending.

"Fine! I'll make my own luck."

The chain at the bottom of the circular staircase

is unhooked, and the shock freezes me in place like a mannequin. "Twiggy? Twiggy, did you unhook the chain?"

"Take it easy, doll. The power just came back on line along Main Street and I have to reset the system to switch from the backup battery to the main power source."

See, I knew she had a backup battery! "All right. I would hate to leave the Rare Books Loft unsecured."

"Don't worry your pretty little head, Your Highness. I've got everything under control."

Striding to the back room in my grosgrain-ribbon wedges, I strike a Hepburn-esque pose and wait for her to turn.

She does not.

"I'm headed out to the casino, to follow up on Leticia's murder. Do you need me to grab anything while I'm out?"

Now she creaks around in her rickety rolly chair and fixes me with a baffled stare. "What on earth is that getup?"

"Don't blame me! This is what Grams picked out."

"You look more like you're headed to *Breakfast at Tiffany's* than a meeting at a two-bit casino."

"Hey, movie references are kinda my thing, but

good one. Do you think I can get my Jeep out of the alley?"

She sighs and shrugs. "If you're asking me if the roads are clear, seems like Artie's ahead of schedule on that count. If you're asking me if I have any faith in your driving skills, you probably don't want to hear the answer."

I refuse to take the bait. "Have a lovely afternoon."

Her cackle follows to the alleyway. I'm happy to slam the heavy metal door shut and hurry to the garage.

The roads are clear as far as Gunnison Avenue, and not much has changed since my father drove us back from the marina. There is a fairly obvious track around debris and in and out of the shallow ditches on either side of the road. Traffic is light, and I make it to the casino early.

They must have some massive generators out here. The marquee is glaring its blazing wattage into the afternoon sky, and the parking lot boasts at least fifty cars.

When I enter through the revolving door, the dings, clangs, and flashes of the one-armed bandits assault my senses. They no longer allow smoking inside the establishment—but the olfactory evidence lingers.

Last time I visited the casino, I received an unrequested escort to Leticia Whitecloud's office. The place may be under new management, but I'm willing to bet the head honcho moved right into her ready-made digs.

Closing my eyes briefly, I fast-forward through that memory clip and retrace my steps.

Oddly, the two sets of security guards at either end of the enclosed walkways make no move to stop me. This costume is really working.

Approaching the door to the office, one last wise guy stands in my way.

I open my mouth to announce myself, but he's already twisting the handle and opening the door. My bravado fades as the man behind the desk rises to greet me.

Everything about the place has changed. Gone are the light birchwood furnishings and white leather pieces. Brooding mahogany paired with heavy cordovan chairs and a somber sofa have replaced everything.

"Miss Moon, won't you have a seat." The clipped British accent offers the invitation as a statement, not a question. "I'm Mr. Burwell. Charmed, I'm sure."

The antique mood ring on my left hand burns, but there's no time for it. I have to keep my wits about me and stand my ground now that I'm face to face with the legendary August Burwell. I'm sure

Jimmy will be thrilled to know he's alive. "Thank you, Mr. Burwell, but I won't be here that long. Why don't you tell me about your relationship with the deceased?"

His face blanches, and he drops into his plush leather armchair. "I beg your pardon? Deceased? Of whom do you speak?"

Wow. This guy is good. "Are you going to sit there and pretend that you had no idea your girlfriend Leticia Whitecloud has been murdered?"

The shock on his face shifts to crimson anger. "How dare you impugn me? I have crews searching for her now. I held out hope of life. When that horrible storm upturned our vessel . . ." He places a hand on his desk to steady himself, and motions to a man in the corner who had completely escaped my awareness.

The anvil-armed Native American who steps from the shadows is built to inflict maximum damage. He's obviously a bodyguard, but as I observe him pour bourbon into an old-fashioned glass over a single sphere of ice, I take it he fills more than one slot on the employee roster.

"Let's say your statement about the boat accident is true. How is it you arrived here at the casino without a scratch?"

"Why, I stepped into the lifeboat Jimmy offered. I merely assumed he had already seen to the welfare of Ms. Whitecloud, as that is his primary function."

"Interesting. Why would one of your own employees inform me that there were no lifeboats on the floating casino?"

"I must admit, I don't know."

Great. The more witnesses I interview, the more conflicting stories I get. "I happen to know the Tribal Council wrested control of the casino from Ms. Whitecloud last year. If you're connected to her, why am I finding you in this office?"

"I am simply a manager, contracted by the Council to set operations right."

"And your involvement with the previous manager?"

He stands, straightens his pocket square, and glances briefly at his hulking protector. "I don't appreciate your insinuation, Miss Moon. Theodore will see you out."

Scenes from a variety of vigilante movies flash through my mind, but the montage ends with my grandmother's disappointed visage scowling as she shakes a finger toward me. Any bright ideas I had about going all *The Long Kiss Goodnight* and demanding answers vanish in the face of her stern reproach. "Thank you, Mr. Burwell. I can find my own way out."

I tug my arm from Theodore's grasp, turn on my wedge-heeled sandals, and strut out of the casino.

What a conundrum! Either this guy's lying, Jimmy's lying, or that scrawny little server is lying.

Or maybe they're all lying! Nothing would surprise me at this point.

As I approach my Jeep in the parking lot, the mood ring burns with an undeniable fire. I look down and see my Jeep.

"Spoiler alert, unhelpful ring, I'm already aware that my Jeep is in the parking lot."

When I utter the word Jeep out loud, the hairs on the back of my neck tingle and I sense a presence inside the vehicle.

I've seen way too many movies and television shows to ignore this series of warnings. Rather than sliding blindly into the driver's seat to be strangled, I unlock the vehicle, open the passenger-side rear door, and hop in. "You've got exactly five seconds to explain yourself, before my itchy trigger finger finds relief."

The barrel of my loaded weapon is trained directly at the huddled mass on the floor, wedged between the driver's seat and the back bench seat.

"Don't shoot! Please, don't shoot. I need help."

There's something about that voice. "Aren't you that server? Busboy, whatever?"

The familiar face looks up. His dark eyes are

wild with fright. "Someone was in my apartment. The door was kicked in and the whole place was trashed. I think it's a warning."

"And what would this warning be in reference to, Tripp?"

"The stuff I told you. About the lifeboats and, you know."

"So you stand by your claim."

His expression shifts from fear to confusion. "Claim? There were no lifeboats. Why would I lie? Check with the Coast Guard, or whoever. Can't be that hard to find out." He gasps for air and lurches forward.

I slide away from him and re-aim my gun. "I'm serious about shooting you. Somebody's lying to me, and that makes me highly suspicious."

He braces himself on the transmission tunnel and lifts his other hand in the air. "Hold on. I swear, I don't have a gun. I can't breathe on account of my asthma. Seriously, there were no lifeboats. Can I please grab my inhaler?"

"Get in the front seat."

"No way. Shoot me, I guess, but I'm not gonna let them see me talking to you. The first time was a warning. You know the next time they'll kill me."

All right, Mitzy. Pay attention to your own psychic messages. This kid is legitimately terrified. He believes what he's telling you is true, and, what's more, he has absolutely nothing to gain by falsely accusing Jimmy of this murder.

"Fine. Get your inhaler and lie down on the back seat. I'm driving you directly to the sheriff's station. They'll place you in protective custody, and I'm going to finish my investigation. If you're lying to me, you'll already be in custody. If you're telling the truth, they're the only ones who can protect you."

"Okay, sure. Whatever you say. I'm too freaked to argue."

Extrasensory perceptions confirmed. This kid has to be innocent.

I step out of the vehicle, make a show of collecting trash from the floorboards and walking to a trash can outside the entrance, before reentering my vehicle on the driver's side. I know they have security cameras everywhere. That performance may not throw them off the scent permanently, but hopefully it will give us time to get across the isthmus before they can shut down the bridge.

On the way back toward Pin Cherry, I call my boyfriend. "Sheriff Harper—"

He interrupts me with a wiseacre remark concerning my use of his formal title and goes on to explain what my punishment could involve.

While his offer is beyond enticing, I'm grateful this convo is not on speaker. I force the conversation back on track. "As I was saying, Sheriff Harper. I'm bringing in a crucial witness in the Whitecloud murder. He's requesting to be placed in protective custody until the case is solved."

Erick instantly switches gears and promises to make the necessary arrangements.

Call ends.

"Everything will be taken care of by the time we arrive at the station. Is there anything else you can tell me? Where was August Burwell before the storm hit?"

"Who?"

"Leticia's boyfriend."

"Oh, the snooty British guy?"

"The very one."

"He was at the bar on the second level, near the front of the boat. Or the prow, I think. He was totally trashed."

Glancing in the rearview mirror, I narrow my gaze. "The boat had barely left the marina. How could the guy be drunk?"

"Maybe he had some pre-party beers. How should I know? He was talking loud about what a great gambler he was, slurring his words, and spilling booze all over."

Now there's an interesting tidbit. I've played drunk on more than one occasion. When you only have enough money in your pocket for one or two drinks, you learn how to make them last all night, and make sure your friends think you're wasted. Of course, I would never spill my drink, but birds of a feather . . . I think Sir Snooty Pants is guilty of more than fake inebriation.

CHAPTER 11

THE UNIVERSE IS SMILING down upon us. The road is clear and there's a parking space right in front of the station. Easing in, I make an announcement. "Last stop."

"Are you sure they can protect me?"

Turning in my seat in order to peer over my right shoulder, I whip off my designer shades and frown. "Have you got a better idea, fugitive?"

He shrugs his narrow shoulders.

"Then come with me if you want to live." I'll admit, my Arnold Schwarzenegger impersonation is weak, but it gets a small grin from my nervous passenger.

He steps out of the vehicle, and I join him on the sidewalk.

The deputy I've nicknamed Furious Monkeys

occupies her standard spot at the front desk, and the look of concentration on her face indicates she's deep into the world of virtual primates.

"Hey, Deputy Baird. What level are you now?"

She doesn't pull her eyes away from the screen, but a smile flickers across her face. "Hit 268 this morning. Last month I thought I had the game beat —250 was the highest—then they released thirty new levels."

"Good for you. Did Erick mention I was bringing in a witness?"

"Right. The protective custody thing?"

"10-4."

She jerks her thumb toward the bullpen. "You'll want to talk to Paulsen."

If she thinks for one minute that I have ever in my life *wanted* to talk to Deputy Paulsen, she is sadly mistaken. "Thanks."

Turning to my charge, I motion for him to follow as I push through the crooked swinging gate and walk, with a confidence I don't possess, toward the portly, trigger-happy deputy's desk.

"What's this one guilty of?"

"At this point, he doesn't appear to be guilty of anything. He has valuable information in the Whitecloud murder case, and someone broke into his place to try to frighten him into keeping quiet."

She hoists herself to her feet, adjusts the duty

belt cinched around her doughy middle, and, as always, places her right hand on her gun. "Is that so?"

The kid nods.

"I'll take it from here, Moon. You can go ahead and leave the real police work to the professionals."

Her condescending remarks used to get under my skin, but now every time she lashes out at me, I remind myself that she's lost two elections to my boyfriend, and my grandmother personally made the largest donation on record to his last campaign. I may stifle my comeback, but I can't keep the smug grin from my face. "Best of luck to you then."

She scoffs, spits in her trash can, and grips the witness by the arm, as though he were a suspect.

"Is Erick—"

She rudely interrupts. "*Sheriff Harper* is out of the station."

I tip my floppy brim in her direction and exit before I say something I'll enjoy, but Erick will regret.

On the brief drive back to my bookshop, I reach out to Sheriff Too-Hot-To-Handle. "Hey, can you check on something for me?"

He agrees to do me a favor if it can be handled over the phone.

"I need to find out, for certain, if the Hawk Island Floating Casino was equipped with lifeboats."

He informs me that Whitecloud somehow obtained "moored barge" status for the vessel, which places it in a classification that wouldn't be required by the Coast Guard to carry them.

"Are you sure?"

He inhales sharply.

"Skip that. I'm just a little confused. Jimmy said he was helping people into lifeboats. August Burwell, the new manager of the land-based casino, also tells a story involving boats. The only person challenging their story is this scrawny server who was admittedly working his first gig aboard Leticia's gambling ship."

The sheriff suggests the kid could be mistaken or confused.

"Sure, he could be wrong. But if he is, why is someone trying to keep him quiet?"

Erick offers to make a few phone calls to confirm the gambling ship's kit, and I shove the phone in my straw handbag with extreme frustration.

Something is not right. I need Grams to snap out of her funk and help me run through potential scenarios on the boat. As I walk down the alley toward the metal door, a strange idea works its way to my consciousness. What if no one's lying?

Good one brain! I'm sure there's any number of options that would lead to completely conflicting stories coexisting in my universe. Throwing my hands in the air with a sigh, I open the side door and check for my employee. "Twiggy? You still here?"

There's no reply, but I sense something.

Quietly taking the gun from my bag, I set the straw purse on the floor and inch along the wall to the back room.

Someone—or is it two someones?—is definitely in the back room.

Leaning against the wall, I close my eyes and reach out. If psychic confirmation counts for anything, there are two heartbeats right around the corner.

I choose to lean into my innocence, and tuck the weapon in the back of my waistband. Stumbling through the doorway, I screech to a halt and hope my acting skills pass muster. "What's going on?"

Twiggy's dilapidated chair is turned toward me, and Jimmy stands behind it with his weapon pressed against her temple.

Despite the circumstances, my volunteer employee appears unruffled.

"I need some answers—now."

"And you'll get them. I'm working *with* you, Jimmy. There's no need for you to threaten my employee."

His hulking shoulders relax a fraction, but he doesn't holster the gun.

"You must have quite an armory at home. I remember relieving you of a couple guns less than twenty-four hours ago."

"I don't have time for your smart mouth. I need to know who killed her."

I hate to bargain with someone else's life, but the unshakable nerves of my grandmother's dearest friend will surely hold up. "You put the gun away, and we'll sit down and have a civilized conversation."

He leans forward and his nostrils flare. "Where's the waiter?"

"Everyone disembarked at the marina, just like you."

His voice dips an octave, and the gravelly threat makes Twiggy's eyes widen. "I'm not playing games, kid. Where's the waiter?"

That's it. I wasn't born with patience, and I will not start getting them now. Quick as a flash, I snatch the gun from my waistband and aim it directly at his head. "I'm a little rusty, but I think this could be a Mexican standoff. Put down your gun and have a seat. I'll answer any questions you want, but Twiggy walks out of here—now."

Maybe it's the extrasensory perceptions, or maybe it's just women's intuition, but I think my stoic coworker is approaching her tipping point.

He exhales, flicks the safety on his pistol, and shoves it in his holster. "Satisfied?"

"Halfway there. Twiggy, can you check on Pyewacket?"

She swallows hard and slides out of the chair. "You got it."

There was no "doll," no "kid," and no "your highness." She hustles out of the back room like a house on fire.

"Have a seat, Jimmy. Can I get you something to drink?"

He scowls and scrapes a chair back from the small bistro table.

I pull the chair closest to me about two feet away from the table, take a seat and re-aim my weapon center mass.

"You can put that away. I was only trying to get your attention. I would never hurt Twiggy."

"Sorry, buddy. You lost the right to insist on my trust when you threatened someone close to me. Ask your questions. You're free to go whenever you want. This gun, however, is going nowhere."

He looks at the gun and clearly recognizes it as the one my father and I relieved him of at the wake all those months ago. "Nice piece. If memory serves, it pulls to the left."

"Thanks. I'll keep that in mind. Now what is so important that you came in here guns drawn?"

"Burwell's missing. Leticia's dead. And some

sniveling minimum-wage punk is pointing the finger at me."

"What makes you say that?" Interesting. Apparently word of Burwell's survival hasn't spread.

He slams his hand down on the table, and I'm thankful I kept my finger next to the trigger rather than on it. Or he'd be seriously wounded.

"Burwell thought he had me snowed. Leticia let her guard down. I told her that guy was no good the minute he sidled up and promised to give her a cut of the casino business if she left quietly."

I sniff and tilt my head back. "I always wondered how the Tribal Council got rid of her so easily."

He shakes off my accusation. "She had her hands in everything. Even if they pushed her out of the tribe's official casino, she was still getting a cut of the race track—"

"I'm aware of her exploits. We're not here to memorialize a criminal. You claimed to have urgent questions."

"Right. The kid. I heard someone from the crew told you there were no lifeboats. Don't think I didn't notice you getting friendly with him on the yacht."

Best if I avoid addressing that accusation head-on. "Why would that matter? Whether or not there were lifeboats is easy enough to confirm with the Coast Guard, right?"

He rolls his shoulders back and crosses his arms. "Not as easy as you might think. The paperwork for that vessel isn't a hundred percent above board. And I wasn't helping passengers into a lifeboat. I was helping Burwell and his muscle—"

"I thought Leticia Whitecloud was your number one priority. You mean to tell me, there was a deadly storm bearing down on her main source of income, and you were helping her rival escape?" I shake my head. "Then you should be thrilled to hear that I met with Mr. Burwell, alive and well, out at the casino no more than thirty minutes ago."

Jimmy scowls. "So he ain't missing?"

"Nope. Call me crazy, but I still don't get why you helped him and not Leticia?"

"This was before the sirens. The radio was on the fritz when we boarded. Leticia insisted the storm would blow itself out long before it got to Pin Cherry. We had no idea how bad it was getting. She knew there was a throng of tourists waiting to gamble. People drink more when a storm's brewing. They drink more, then they bet more."

"Holy *Hurricane Heist*!" I shake my head in disbelief. "She knowingly put her employees in harm's way so she could bilk some tourists?"

His thick arms fall to his sides, and he sucks air between his teeth. "Business before all. That was her motto."

"Nice boss. I can't say I'm sorry she's gone."

He leans forward menacingly. "You should be. She's a damn angel of mercy compared to Burwell. You have no idea what that man is capable of."

"Is he capable of murder, Jimmy?"

Jimmy nods and his massive shoulders droop. "Without hesitation."

The side door bangs open and footsteps thunder in our direction.

"Where is he?"

"Dad?"

My father rounds the corner with the fury of an enraged grizzly bear. "I save your kid's life down in Clearwater, more than once, and this is how you repay me. Holding my little girl at gunpoint?"

Jimmy lifts both of his hands in the air. "Easy, Duncan. She's the one pointing a gun at me."

My dad hesitates in confusion, and I jump to my feet to let the rest of the wind out of his sails. "It's true. He didn't point the gun at me. He was holding Twiggy hostage, but he never pointed the gun at me."

My father clocks the gun in my hand, looks back at Jimmy and clenches his jaw. "Don't you ever set foot in this bookshop again."

Goosebumps pop up all over my arms, and, not for the first time, I'm thankful Jacob Duncan is on my side.

Jimmy gets to his feet and nods solemnly. "Sorry for the trouble. I didn't mean any disrespect."

My dad crosses his arms and puffs out his barrel chest. "Just remember who owes who, Jimmy. Maybe you should take this opportunity to turn your life around. I've got a stack of job opportunities on my desk for someone like you."

Jimmy steps past us and pauses in the hallway. "I've lived this life too long, Duncan. The things I've done . . . I can never make it on an honest man's salary."

The surge of adrenaline fueling my father's protective instincts has dissipated, and his underlying mission to find jobs for ex-cons takes center stage. "Don't give up on yourself."

Jimmy scoffs, looks at the floor, and exits without a word.

One crisis handled. Now for the next infraction. "Twiggy! Did you call my dad?"

She steps out from between the stacks, her standard air of superiority restored. "I know you think you're pretty hot stuff with the pistol, doll, but it never hurts to have backup."

"Are you sure you're okay?" My father grips my shoulders and searches my face desperately.

"I'm fine. I totally had things under control."

"You shouldn't have that gun, Mitzy. Take it

from someone who knows. Carrying a gun only ever ends badly. I'd take it from you, but you know what they say about felons and firearms."

Rubbing his shoulder, I offer a compromise. "I'll only use it as a last resort."

My father shakes his head as a horrible memory flashes behind his eyes. "Put it away. Or it might be your last, last resort."

"Copy that. Um, can you hang on a minute? I'm gonna run upstairs and put this away, but I need to ask you some questions."

He nods, walks to the sink, and grabs a glass from the drying rack. "Sure thing. I'll be right here with my glass of 'calm down water' when you get back."

Hustling upstairs, I give Grams a condensed update and promise to fill her in later.

Returning to the back room, I seek advice. "It feels like everyone's lying to me. That's impossible, right?"

"Not entirely. What's going on?"

"That server who talked to me when we were bringing the survivors back to the marina is being threatened. Someone broke into his place and tossed it as some kind of warning."

"Warning for what? He didn't actually see anything, did he?" Jacob takes a sip of water.

"I suppose not. But *not* seeing Jimmy on the

boat sounds pretty incriminating. If Jimmy wasn't on the boat, what was he up to?" Leaning back in the chair, I toss my hat on the table and fluff my hair.

My father places his elbows on the table and leans forward. "Hold on. If Jimmy wasn't on the casino boat, how did he get over to the island?"

"Yeah, that's a good point, too. I think we need a list of all the crewmembers. I want to see if their stories match."

"Can you ask Erick to round them up?" He swipes a drip of water from his mouth.

"He's already burning the candle at both ends. If Jimmy's as innocent as he says, maybe he can get me the names."

Jacob bites his lip and shakes his head. "And if he isn't innocent, you're gonna put a lot of potential victims in his sight line. The Duncan name still carries a lot of weight around the waterfront. Let me see if I can get you the name of the captain and you can take it from there."

"Thanks, Dad. You make a good sidekick."

He chuckles and gets to his feet. "Sidekick? At the very least, you should bill me as the muscle." He slams his right fist into his open left palm.

"No joke. That was a definite movie-trailer-worthy entrance."

He nods his head. "I have a lot of lost time to

make up for. Nobody's gonna mess with my little girl on my watch."

"I appreciate the sentiment, Dad. Really, I do. But could you refer to me as your daughter, rather than a little girl? I am twenty-three, you know."

He bends and kisses the top of my head. "Whatever you say, princess."

Groaning audibly, I roll my eyes. "That's worse!"

He chuckles and heads for the side door. "I'll give you a ring if I find any information."

"Sounds good."

Retrieving the hat from the table, I exhale loudly. That's enough excitement for one day. I'm going to update my murder board and grab a to-go lasagna from Angelo and Vinci's. Trudging up the wrought-iron staircase, I call out to my wildcat. "Pyewacket, I'm ordering Italian. You want a meatball?"

"RE-ow." Feed me.

CHAPTER 12

PYEWACKET HOLDS THE RECORD for most forced awakenings of this particular human. But today, the award goes to Jacob Duncan.

An unwelcome ringing resounds from the phone on my bedside table. My half-asleep arm swats toward the disturbance and connects with the speaker icon. "This better be good."

My father chuckles. "Don't tell me you're still in bed? With the excitement of this investigation, I thought you'd be up with the sun's first light."

"Give me a break. You and I both know that never happens."

He chuckles. "I got the name of the captain. He's been handling private charters in the area for almost two decades. He piloted more than one of your grandmother's exclusive parties, and her habit of hefty tips left an impression. As soon as I mentioned my name, he offered me the crew roster with no argument."

"Sweet!"

"I asked him to meet you down at the marina, next to our slip. I know it's a small town, and I'm sure he knows you own the bookshop, but it didn't feel right giving out my baby girl's personal address."

"Dad! I'm a grown woman!"

"You sound more like a caged wildcat. You better meet me down at the diner for breakfast and coffee!"

"No time. My to-do list is longer than Rapunzel's hair. I'm gonna brew a cup of subpar coffee downstairs and steal some Fruity Puffs."

A needle-clad paw thwacks my leg, and the thin summer comforter offers little protection. "Ouch! Stop being a bully, Pye."

The tan terror refuses to open his eyes, but offers a low warning growl.

My father is chuckling on the other end of the line. "Sounds like you're taking a terrible risk. Update me later. And let me know if you need any help with those interviews."

"Copy that. Thanks for the intel."

"Put it on my tab."

"Ha ha." Ending the call, I push myself to a

seated position and yawn extra loud. "Time to rise and flicker."

Grams calls out from the closet. "Can I come with you today?"

She's still struggling with her decision whether to stay in the amulet or risk crossing over if she agrees to let Silas free her. "Sure. It might be your last excursion outside the bookshop, right?"

She mumbles a moody reply.

"Give me a hot minute to get changed, and then it's teamwork time."

That gets the response I had hoped for. "Oh, Mitzy! You're such a hoot."

My feline overlord strongly disagrees. Pyewacket crouches low in the corner of the back room, and his tail thumps rhythmically on the floor as he glares at my breakfast.

"It's only a handful of your special cereal. I promise I'll stop by the Piggly Wiggly and get three more boxes. My mission in life is to make sure you are never out of Fruity Puffs."

"Reow." Can confirm.

Grams giggles at her entitled feline. "Mr. Cuddlekins is such a little sweetie pie."

"False." Finishing the swill that passes for java in this place, I check my text messages for the captain's phone number, and fire off an invite.

He agrees to meet me in thirty minutes.

"You better take some cash, dear."

"How's that now?"

"You heard your father. The man has grown accustomed to the Duncan's generous tips. I'm sure he's not providing the list of names pro bono."

"He should, though! Once again your overindulgence rolls downhill."

She giggles uncontrollably. "That's not the only thing that rolls downhill, sweetie." Grams continues snickering while I march upstairs and retrieve a fistful of cash from my bureau drawer.

Ages ago, when I didn't have enough coin to keep the lights on in my apartment, it would've been beyond my wildest dreams to have a drawer full of cash. Now that I live in the town that tech forgot, it seems as natural as the sun rising every morning. I've come a long way, baby.

"You really have. You're absolutely the best granddaughter I could ever imagine."

"Ah, Grams. That's so sweet it almost makes me forget about you breaking the rules. But not quite. If you're going to come with me today, I'm going to need you to stay out of my business and out of my head. I can't be questioning these crew members and have you spouting off at will."

"I've never spouted in my life. If I have some-thing useful to share, what should I do?"

"Hmmm. How about something totally human?

Maybe you can just offer a soft 'excuse me.' Then patiently wait for me to find the right opportunity to entertain your thoughts."

She makes a sound that's all too similar to Silas and his harrumphs. I choose to ignore the tantrum.

"Hold down the fort, Pyewacket. We'll be back before you know it."

He blinks slowly, in a combination of acknowledgment and boredom.

The bright sun sparkling off the still waters of the marina offers a false sense of calm. Just beyond the neatly aligned slips, recovery operations continue. Boats that can be salvaged are being towed back to dry dock, and personal or professional restoration efforts are underway.

It's my understanding that some of the capsized vessels went down in water too deep for rescue. There's no telling if the tribe or Burwell will make any effort to recover the floating casino. In my opinion, it's nothing more than unnecessary competition for the original casino. But I doubt they give two hoots about my opinion.

A man roughly Odell's age offers a friendly wave as I walk down the dock. "Nelson Perry?"

He salutes me. "The very one. You must be Mitzy Moon. I have a list for you."

"That's what I was told."

He offers me a single sheet of paper, and I hand him several twenties.

Nelson takes the money and smiles. "It's nice to see that the Duncan generosity didn't skip a generation."

Grams sighs with pride. "What did I tell you?"

Clearing my throat, I hope Grams receives the unspoken message. "You bet. I really appreciate the help. Are these phone numbers here correct?"

He glances at the sheet and nods. "Everyone except the new guy."

"I run my finger down the list. Who's this last guy on the list? I thought Tripp Kenosha was the new guy."

"Oh, he was new to the ship, but the guy with no phone number . . . I never seen him around before. He showed up after the drunk one got fired. Some kinda last-minute temp. Maybe somebody else on that list knows him."

"I'll check it out. Thanks." Turning to leave, I stop in my tracks as Grams whispers, "Ask about the lifeboats."

"Hey, can I ask you a question?"

Before he says it, I can tell by the look on his face that it's happening. "Well, technically that already was a question." He laughs at his own clever reply.

I offer a courtesy grin. "Right. I'll get on with it. Was the radio working when you left the marina?"

The corner of his mouth twitches and he blinks rapidly. "The first mate sees to the safety checks."

That answer means he absolutely knew and set off into the lake, regardless. "Of course. And it's my understanding there were no lifeboats on board, is that correct?"

He takes a step backward. "Hey, I was just there to captain the ship. I don't get involved in safety checks or equipment lists."

"I totally understand. It's not an official question or anything. I had heard that some people were getting into a lifeboat, but it's my understanding that moored barges don't need them. Seemed like a weird conflict, you know?"

He nods and takes another half step away. "I didn't see anything like that from the bridge. Again, maybe somebody else on the roster will have some other information. I've got to get going."

"Sure. Don't let me keep you. Thanks for this." I wave the paper and smile.

He turns and hurries down the dock. Unless he's getting on a boat, I have no idea where he's going. The only way back to land is the direction I'm going. He's probably not guilty of anything more than following a criminal's orders, but he obviously has a guilty conscience.

Grams chimes in. "Barely. Can't believe I ever thought so highly of that man. He clearly has no morals."

Back inside my vehicle, I begin the boring task of texting everyone on the list. Rather than charge out of the gate with the notion that I'm investigating a murder, I go with a story that a wallet was recovered containing a considerable sum of money, and I'm trying to get it back to the rightful owner. If it's theirs or they know whom it might belong to, they should text.

Unsurprisingly this ploy works on all but two of the recipients.

After exchanging a series of texts with the folks who do reply, I manage to narrow the list down to three people who saw Jimmy on the boat. And two more folks who saw a single inflatable boat with a small outboard motor, leaving the floating casino shortly after they departed the marina.

I offer to meet these people at half-hour intervals at Myrtle's Diner and insist there's a reward for information leading to the owner of the wallet. Three people agree to meet.

The first girl is Sadie, home from college and working a summer job aboard the floating casino.

She can't seem to stop playing with her own honey-brown locks the entire time she speaks. "So, like I was supposed to serve drinks after we picked up the marks, or whatevs, but then, like, the siren went off and it was just super cray."

My grandmother groans in the amulet.

"I'm sure. Where did you see Jimmy?"

"Oh, yeah, right?" She twists a hunk of hair and adjusts it on her shoulder. "He was, like, coming up from the downstairs deck, or whatever. I mean, maybe he was mad, but it's hard to tell. He's kind of always serious, you know." Flicks the same hunk of hair over her shoulder.

"I do. Did you see him near the lifeboats?"

"No. Like, never. There's no little boats on the big one. So, like, maybe that was a lifeboat, but I don't know what it was." She grips two chunks of what I'm now certain are extensions and smooths them on either side of her cleft chin. "But it looked kind of blowup-ish and like a raft, maybe? That super-hot British guy and his thirst-trap bodyguard, or whatevs, were the only ones I saw by that thing."

Aaaaand both swaths get simultaneously flipped back over her bare shoulders.

"Got it. Thank you so much for your help." I slide some money across the table and her heavily lined eyes widen.

"That's lit. I thought the reward would be like, twenty bucks, you know?"

"I do know. Thanks again for your help. Can I text you if I have more questions?"

"Totally." She collects the cash, shoves it in the front pocket of her booty-shorts and bounces.

Odell lifts an eyebrow and tilts his head. I shrug my shoulders and chuckle.

The next taker is a clean-cut man in his thirties with a noticeable band of white skin on his ring finger. Crikey! This guy better be a divorcé.

Grams scoffs. "I doubt it. Looks like a philanderer if I've ever seen one."

Ew.

"Hey, are you the gal who called about Jimmy?"

"Yes. You said you saw him on the boat?"

His eager energy fades. "Oh, you were serious about that?"

Grams interrupts. "Told you so."

"Yes, I was serious. I'm so sorry if you thought my questions regarding whether or not someone was on a boat and whether that vessel had lifeboats came across as a pickup line. It wasn't. But what you can do is pick yourself up and get out of this diner." I swirl my finger once and point firmly toward the door.

He opens his mouth to defend himself, but I hold that single finger up and press it toward him. "Say it walking, son."

He mumbles what he surely believes is a clever retort under his breath as he heads for the door.

The scrape of a metal spatula stops abruptly,

and I shift my gaze to Odell. He runs his hand through his high and tight grey buzz cut and nods his approval.

I point to the door the cheater just walked through and mouth, "Right?"

The final taker on my "tips for cash" offer is an attractive blonde in her late twenties.

She walks over to my table and smiles. "You're the one who called, right? You said white hair, and for some reason that made me think you would be old, but you're super young. But you are the one who called—"

I interrupt her before she can begin another lap of her circular logic. "I am. Have a seat."

I signal Tally, and she drops off two menus. When I set up this operation, I expected to be eating three lunches. Not that I couldn't, but I'm determined to get at least one.

The girl flips through the menu, widens her eyes, and looks at me. "Do you know if they have any vegan options? I've been totally vegan for five years."

"They have french fries." My monotone reply offers no judgment.

She smiles politely. "Miss?" And waves a tentative hand at Tally.

The flame-red bun of my favorite waitress bobs over to the table. "What can I getcha?"

The girl doesn't make eye contact. "I'm wondering if your produce is locally sourced?"

Tally glances toward me. I shrug, and she turns back to the girl. "It's a little early in the growing season for local produce. We try to buy organic whenever we can. Would you like a salad?"

"Do you have non-GMO dressings?"

I bury my head in my menu and refuse to look at Tally.

Grams is laughing uncontrollably.

"I can make you an oil and vinegar. Would that work?"

The girl sighs, closes the menu, and leans against the red vinyl. "Is this cruelty-free leather?"

My eyes widen, and I wonder if Tally will smack the girl with the back of her order pad. But, ever the professional, she smiles and meets clueless where it lives. "It is. I'll bring you a salad with some of that house-made oil and vinegar. Would you like something besides water to drink?"

The satisfied girl nods and smiles brightly. "Yes. I'd like a Diet Coke."

Grams snorts, and I slap a quick hand over my mouth to keep from gasping out loud.

CHAPTER 13

CLEARLY JIMMY ISN'T BEING COMPLETELY honest with me. For that matter, neither is August Burwell, or the intrepid server. My instinct that everyone is lying to me was strangely accurate. I should learn to follow my instincts more carefully and believe in my abilities. At least I'm fairly certain that's what Silas Willoughby would say.

After Jimmy's recent stunt in my bookshop, I'm not feeling great about meeting him in any sort of remote location. He can haul his dishonest behind over to the patisserie. Then I'll have an opportunity to check in on my favorite chocolate croissants while I cross-examine him.

He picks up my call on the first ring and agrees to meet me. Let's be honest, he didn't really have an option. I pretend to have information. He desperately wants it.

After a quick stop at the bookshop to hang up my protesting Grams amulet, I head out for my meeting.

Out front of Bless Choux, the windows are boarded up, but bright-blue paint on the plywood indicates, "We're open during repairs." If there was any doubt about the accuracy of the hastily painted message, the heavenly aroma of fresh pastry removes it.

"Good morning, Mitzy!" Anne waves from behind the counter.

"I expected to see a line around the corner?"

She shrugs. "It's a tough sell with the windows boarded up, but you know how this town is. The word will spread, and tomorrow we'll be packed to the gills."

Nodding my agreement, I step up to the counter and place my order.

"Sit anywhere you like, dear. I'll bring it out to you."

Jimmy's large frame darkens the doorway a couple of minutes after I take my seat. The boarded-up windows create a gloomy, foreboding atmosphere I've never before experienced in this lovely bakery.

He scans the room for any trouble and scowls

when he sees I've left him the chair with his back to the door.

His disappointment pleases me. Mitzy Moon is no amateur. I've seen the movies. I know how to take the power position.

Leaning into my role, when Anne arrives with my repast, I can't help myself. "Whatever my friend here wants. Put it on my tab."

Jimmy's shoulders hunch forward. "Coffee. Black."

She nods and gazes at me with concern, but scurries behind the counter to grab an additional cup of coffee.

"You said you had info."

"I do. I questioned the rest of the crew from the Hawk Island Floating Casino." My extrasensory perceptions detect an unusual response. I expected surprise, but the soupçon of protectiveness is new.

"And."

Never let it be said that this man is a fascinating conversationalist. "And, several of them remember seeing you on the boat. And one even remembers seeing something that could be mistaken for a lifeboat. Are you ready to tell me the truth, Jimmy?"

He sighs, clenches his fists tightly, and slides his hands back across the table as he leans against his chair. "There's nothing to tell. I was on the boat, just like you said."

"Yeah, I get that. What I'm asking you is, what's going on with this inflatable boat with an outboard motor?"

His discomfort ratchets up at least two notches. "It's not my story to tell."

"Jimmy, as of right now, you're my primary suspect. If you want this investigation to head in a different direction, you need to give me something. Who was in the boat?"

He doesn't need to know that I already have a strong suspicion that the airhead from the crew correctly identified Burwell and his intimidating sidekick.

"You didn't hear this from me. In fact, maybe you keep my name out of this altogether?"

If I didn't know better, I'd say there's a slight pleading tone underneath Jimmy's bravado. Now seems like the perfect time to trust my instincts. "They're planning on publishing the names of all the survivors in the *Pin Cherry Harbor Post* tomorrow. If you want your name left off that list, start talking."

That was indeed the proper carrot.

"All right. All right. You keep my name off that list, though. I have your word?"

A verbal response seems weak, so I give a single firm nod.

"Burwell wouldn't get off the boat before we

left the marina. He said he needed a few more minutes with Leticia. That sorry excuse for a bodyguard told me not to sweat it. Said he had everything handled."

"Wait, are you telling me that August Burwell was the last person to see Leticia alive?"

He also skips a verbal response and offers a simple nod of his head.

Leaning back in the chair, I cross my arms. "So Burwell and Theodore left the ship in some little watercraft Theodore tied to the casino ship before you headed out across the lake?" I make no effort to hide my doubts.

Jimmy nods, but offers no further explanation.

"Let's say I believe you. Did they head out before or after the siren?"

He looks up to the left. If my television education is accurate, he's accessing a genuine memory. "Yeah, before the siren."

"So it wasn't until the siren went off that you knew how serious the storm was?"

Jimmy leans forward. "The radio was out. I told you that already."

"Maybe. Maybe you left that bit out."

He shakes his head. "No, I told you that part. I remember."

"It never hurts to repeat the story. Sometimes you think of things you left out, like this bit about

Burwell's inflatable. Is Theodore part of the local clan, or did Burwell bring him in from outside?"

A hint of nervous energy flashes through the large man across from me. "What does that matter?"

"I could ask you the same thing. If the information is unimportant, why not tell me?"

He exhales with exasperation. "Teddy isn't local, but he's Anishinaabeg. Canadian clan."

"And how did August Burwell get this job opportunity at our local casino?"

Jimmy bites nervously on the inside of his cheek, and his lips twist left and right.

I recognize that move. He's working over the bits of his story, to find out which pieces he can use to both answer the question, and keep me from the truth. "Just tell me the truth. I'm going to find out anyway, and the longer you keep it from me, the more guilty you look."

His face returns to its stoic place of rest, and he takes a shallow breath. "Teddy is my cousin. My ma's sister moved north to separate herself from the scandal—when my son went to prison. She married Teddy's dad, and he's always been loyal to the family."

If loyal to the family means the same thing to this guy as it does to the mafia, I'd say Jimmy is admitting to getting his cousin a shady job and possibly some other shenanigans. "So you arranged for Theodore to work with Burwell?"

"Yeah, I got Teddy the job. Didn't expect him to turn on me."

Despite my concerns about Jimmy's motives, I lean forward, eager to get the rest of the story.

He exhales loudly. "I don't have any proof."

"That doesn't bother me—yet. What's your hunch?"

For the first time since the meeting started, Jimmy feels unsure. I can sense the hesitation and self-doubt. A vibe I've never gotten off this statue of a man before.

"Like I said, it's only a suspicion. I think Burwell was trying to get rid of me."

My eyes widen. "And he killed Leticia, too?"

Jimmy shrugs. "Burwell was skimming roughly a third of the profits from the tribe. He kept two sets of books—the whole deal. Then he'd cut Leticia in for half of his take, and she made sure the right people looked the other way."

"It sounds like the perfect deal, for Leticia. Where do you come in, and why would Burwell care?"

He sighs. "It didn't have anything to do with the money." A heartbreaking sadness ripples across the table and Jimmy presses his lips together. He's working hard to stuff something deep down. My mood ring flashes with heat and the face of Leticia Whitecloud flashes through the mist. "I thought it was odd, you calling her 'Leticia.' You two were involved?"

He nods.

"So when you warned her to stay away from Burwell, it didn't have anything to do with business."

He doesn't respond, but he doesn't need to.

"And now you think Burwell knew about the storm and intended for you to go down with the ship. But somehow you're sure he didn't kill Leticia. How?" Jimmy's energy rapidly shifts to one of protection. "I don't know. Maybe he did. But it doesn't feel right."

I literally run my life off hunches on a daily basis. I can hardly argue with the man. But those very hunches say something else is creeping beneath Jimmy's story. "I'll make sure they keep your name out of the papers, and I won't tell Burwell that we've spoken. I'll be in touch."

He leaves his untouched cup of coffee on the table, scrapes his chair back, and walks to the door. He pauses with a hand pressing against the temporary plywood. "Tell Twiggy I'm real sorry. I was out of line."

I lift my eyebrows and nod. "Accurate."

As soon as the door swishes closed, the owner

steps up with a to-go bag. "Here's a few pastries for you to take. Let Sheriff Harper know we're all grateful for his quick thinking at the festival."

"I will. And thank you for these." I lift the bag and smile. "They won't go to waste."

As I exit into the humidity, a question flies to the forefront. Glancing up and down the street, I catch the unmistakable rumble of a diesel engine.

Running is never my first choice, but I can stomach a brief jog.

Jimmy sees me approaching and puts down his window. "Something on your mind?"

It takes a moment for me to catch my breath, but eventually I gasp out my query. "There was a name on the list with no phone number." I have to close my eyes to visualize the name at the bottom of the list handed to me by the captain. "Do you have a number for Tom Sawyer?"

The muscles in Jimmy's jaw flex. "Nope. Never heard of him." Without waiting for a follow-up question, he puts his lifted truck in gear and guns it toward Main Street.

As soon as I said the name out loud, all the bells went off in my head. Tom Sawyer? Really? If that isn't a fake name, I don't know what is. Now I'm curious if they're a Mark Twain fan or a Rush groupie.

Meandering down Third Avenue, swinging my bag of pastries like a B-list movie star, I can't stop the image of the knife in Leticia's back from flooding in.

There's no denying the symbolism. The person who murdered Leticia Whitecloud was sending a clear message. She stabbed someone in the back, and they were returning the favor. It's not exactly a favor, I suppose.

Jimmy is the scorned lover in this triangle, and that gives him motive and opportunity.

I need to have another chat with August Burwell, but I'd like to loop my hunky lawman into my inquiry.

Conveniently, I look up to discover I'm passing Rex's Drugstore.

Next stop: sheriff's station. Home away from home of my yummy boyfriend.

The sight of Erick walking down the sidewalk toward me causes momentary aphasia.

"Hey! I stopped by the bookshop to check in on you. Twiggy told me—"

"Geez!" Before he can launch into any kind of lecture, I have to put a stop to this. "Twiggy is turning into a real blabbermouth."

He slips his arms around my waist and gives me a quick kiss on the lips before stepping back. "I'm glad she told me about what went down with Jimmy. I'm sure you weren't planning on telling me."

"You don't know that. I might've told you —eventually."

He nods knowingly. "Yep. That's the Mitzy Moon I know."

"I handled things with Jimmy. And I just met with him at the bakery, and everything's cool between us." I lift up the little white bag, and the luscious aromas waft toward him.

He takes the offering, peers inside the bag, and nods appreciatively. "You're not going to be able to bribe your way out of an update."

"I can't believe you think I'd stoop to such levels." We both laugh at that lame argument. "The truth is, I sort of hit a wall. I need backup—like, official backup."

He inhales sharply. "What crazy scheme are you cooking up now?"

"Can you drive me out to the casino and help me interrogate August Burwell? Spoiler alert, I've already been there once on my own, and I promise to tell you everything on the drive."

Wiping the beads of sweat from his brow, he steps under the awning at Rex's. "Let me check in with dispatch and see if they can spare me for an hour."

While he takes care of his business, like a responsible adult, I sneak a chocolate croissant out of the lovely paper sack, and gobble it down like an insolent child.

Erick reaches out and brushes a crumb from my chin with his thumb. "I'll drive you, but if I get a call, we have to leave immediately. No questions asked. Got it?"

"10-4, Sheriff."

Releasing a comic exhale, he shakes his head and gestures to his patrol car as he adds, "Your chariot awaits, milady."

I feign a curtsy and lob the volley right back in his court. "As you were, plebe."

He chuckles all the way to the car, and I keep my promise. On the way out to the casino, I share all the intel I have. Even the bit about the suspicious pseudonym on the crew list.

CHAPTER 14

WHEN YOU WALK into a casino with the local sheriff at your side, it's a completely different experience from walking in as a well-dressed heiress.

Heads turn, several people slink into the shadows, and the security personnel manning the walkways instantly stop us in our tracks.

"You have no jurisdiction here, Sheriff."

"Understood. I'm not here to stir up any trouble. Miss Moon and I would like to have a word with Mr. Burwell, and then we'll be on our way. Sound good?"

One security officer continues to block our path with his arms firmly crossed, while his doppelgänger makes a quick call on a cell.

After an obvious nonverbal cue from the guy on

the phone, our welcoming committee rolls out the red carpet. "Mr. Burwell will see you now."

Doors open without hesitation, but they don't leave us to our own devices. This pair escorts us to the next pair, and they deliver us to the familiar office.

"Come in. Come in, Sheriff. Always a pleasure to cooperate with local law enforcement." Mr. Burwell gestures to the two luxurious leather chairs in front of his desk and casually takes a seat.

Looking over my shoulder, I take in the man positioned unobtrusively in the corner. Now that I know Theodore's back story, I can appreciate his physicality in a new light. The broad shoulders and powerful arms must come from the matriarchs. If Teddy's and Jimmy's mothers are sisters, that explains the similarities. Teddy is at least fifteen years younger than Jimmy, and it makes sense that Jimmy would look out for his cousin.

Theodore avoids my eyes and his hands are clasped together in front of his vitals, like a soccer player defending against a free kick.

Taking my seat next to Erick, I lean back and smile broadly. "Good to see you again, August. I've spoken to the crew; those who survived, that is." No need to tell him they all survived. Let him wonder about Jimmy a bit longer. "And I had some additional questions."

My extra senses pick up on his hidden concerns, but his exterior is all calm and cooperation. "Of course. Anything I can do to assist in solving this heinous crime. Ms. Whitecloud will be sorely missed, I'm sure."

Swallowing the snarky reply dancing on the tip of my tongue, I attempt to use my grandmother's technique for catching more flies with honey. "I can certainly see why the Council chose you to take over operations here. Clearly, you have as much concern for the community as they do."

He nods, but I sense he's keeping up his guard. "Is there a reason you brought the sheriff, Miss Moon?"

"Right, sorry about that. As you know, I'm looking into this for my own reasons. I knew Leticia well. However, if I come across something that could help the sheriff and his homicide investigation . . . Well, it's a timesaver, I guess."

His laughter rings hollow in my ears. He's not amused, but Burwell seems to buy the story. "Certainly. Proceed, my dear."

"Thank you. Can you tell me about the small craft you and Theodore used to depart the Hawk Island Floating Casino, prior to the tornado siren?"

Two distinct sensations hit me simultaneously. Erick is stifling his amusement at my left-field approach, and Burwell is struggling to put together an answer that won't incriminate him.

"Are you referring to the lifeboats?"

Interesting stall tactic. "I don't think so. I'm no mariner, but it's my understanding that Leticia had classified the floating casino in some way that exempted it from carrying lifeboats. And I wasn't referring to 'boats,' plural. Based on eyewitness reports, there was only one inflatable boat with a small outboard motor. You and—" I gesture over my shoulder to Teddy. "You and your assistant were the only ones seen leaving."

A rustle behind me makes the hairs on the back of my neck tingle.

However, a quick warning glance from Sheriff Harper settles Theodore's concerns.

"Oh, certainly. With the stress of the natural disaster, and loss of property in the community, my thoughts must have become muddled. Theodore and I were due back at the casino to welcome visiting elders from a Canadian clan."

"Understood. Was there a reason you remained on the vessel in the first place, rather than disembark before they departed the marina?"

His mouth works hard to maintain decorum. "Simply business. I'm sure you understand."

"I think I do. I understand that you and Leticia

had an arrangement. If stories can be believed, maybe more than one."

Teddy steps forward, and Erick stands to face him. "No need to escalate this friendly chat."

Burwell gives a curt nod, and Teddy returns to his corner.

"I'm not sure what you heard, Miss Moon, but Ms. Whitecloud and I had a working relationship. I am new to casino operations, and she kindly consulted when necessary."

"Interesting. So you weren't aware of the severity of the storm?"

This question brings a spike to his heart rate. And my eager clairaudience picks up the word bouncing around his brain. *Radio.*

"Did you know about the radio on board the gambling vessel?"

He fidgets in his chair and rubs his hand from his earlobe across his neck, before crossing his arms firmly over his chest. "I was merely a passenger. I had no interaction with the captain or any safety checks."

"Right. However, the captain didn't seem to remember doing safety checks either. He assigned that to the first mate." I twist in my chair and stare at Theodore. "Teddy, did you know something about the radio?"

His black eyes burn with anger, and he narrows his gaze.

Now that I have everyone's undivided attention, it seems like the perfect time to stick a toothpick in this cake. I realize it's a terrible analogy, but I'm short on seafaring knowledge. Ooooh, wait! Maybe this is a keel-hauling situation.

Erick leans toward me. "Was there more to your story, Moon?"

"What? Right. Yes." I clear my throat dramatically and continue. "Let me tell you what I think happened, Mr. Burwell. Teddy visited the casino ship as soon as you heard about the big storm. He disabled the radio and paid off the captain. You were tired of cooking the books only to lose half of the profits you were skimming to Leticia. You saw an opportunity to take her out of the equation and let the storm cover your tracks."

He leans forward to argue, but I hold out my hand.

"Hold on. Not quite finished. I think you also knew that Jimmy Blackburn would be on board, and you took out two birds with one storm." I'm secretly very pleased at how I was able to twist that idiom to my will.

He gets to his feet, and Erick's hand slips carefully toward his gun.

"Don't do anything stupid, Burwell. I may not

have specific jurisdiction here, but I will intervene if I feel lives are threatened."

The swirl of anger behind me is gaining strength, much like the deadly twister that hit earlier this week.

Burwell stares down Sheriff Harper. "This conversation is over. You and this amateur can leave now, of your own free will, or test my patience and let Theodore remove you."

Erick nods. "We're happy to leave. I'll be contacting Tribal Council and arranging for your extradition. If you think for a moment they're going to protect someone who is stealing from the tribe, you're sadly mistaken."

Theodore rushes forward and, instead of drawing his weapon, Erick picks up one of the heavy office chairs and launches it directly into Teddy's breadbasket.

The bodyguard hunches over, unable to catch his breath. Erick pulls out his cuffs and moves to take advantage of his brilliant maneuver.

Meanwhile, my extra senses get hit with another strategy entirely. August Burwell is going for a gun in his desk.

Running around the massive mahogany desk will take too much time, and give Burwell an opportunity I don't want him to have. In a flash, I opt to Luke Duke myself across his desk, crash into him in classic klutz form, and we both tumble to the floor.

He may be good looking and British, but I'm scrappy. I have the upper hand, and possibly a slight weight advantage, but I'm not focusing on that.

Erick steps forward. "The rules of the game just changed, Burwell. I'm going to check that top drawer, and if there's a gun in it, you and Teddy are coming with me—now. Pulling a gun on the local sheriff, even on tribal lands, is frowned upon in Pin Cherry." He tugs Teddy with him, and I open the drawer. A pristine Walther PPK lies in the drawer.

The sheriff takes a quick photo, stows his phone, and tosses me a spare pair of handcuffs.

I happily slap the cuffs on Burwell.

As we approach the office door, my quarry sputters uncontrollably. "Wait, wait, wait. Theodore was only doing his job. I'll tell you what you want to know. I didn't kill her. This I swear to you. I would never lift a finger to harm that woman."

There is some truth in his words, but there's something slimy just below the surface.

Erick pauses, tilts his head, and smiles. "You have sixty seconds to change my mind."

Burwell twists his wrists in the handcuffs. "Can you take these off?"

Chuckling, I reply, "Nope. Say your piece."

"Such hostility. Fine. I instructed Theodore to disable the radio. I had no idea the storm would be so severe. Locals assured me that no significant tornadoes had ever struck this far north. You see, Leticia and I had had a tiff. I believed a few hours bouncing around on stormy seas would clear her head. But I had no intention of killing her, nor covering any tracks." He looks down his nose at me. "Clearly this uncouth woman does not understand the finer points of a business relationship."

Without blowing Jimmy's cover, there's not much more I can say. But all my special powers confirm Mr. Burwell's statement is mostly true.

Erick looks at me and casually arches one eyebrow.

Pleased with our evolving nonverbal communication, I take the lead. "And why were you on the boat, Burwell? If you and Leticia were fighting, and you knew the radio had been disabled, why stay aboard?"

For the first time Teddy speaks, and his voice is breathtaking. It has the deep resonance of a classic radio announcer, coupled with the refinement of a Victorian girl fresh from a finishing school. "Mr. Burwell was in attendance to ensure the voyage took place. When the first mate discovered trouble with the radio, there was talk of scuttling the trip. Mr. Burwell informed me he intended to embark with the vessel, to reassure Leticia and the crew. He endeavored to make her believe he had put their differences aside, while I lashed the small inflatable to the starboard side."

The mirror of shock on Erick's face confirms I'm not the only one utterly gobsmacked by Theodore's speech. After that, I'm not sure I'll ever feel comfortable calling him Teddy again—far too pedestrian for such a man. "And once you were in the harbor, you made your escape. Where was Jimmy when this happened?"

There it is. The flash of tension. The unspoken thing they're hiding beneath their confession.

Burwell answers. "I believe he was—"

Theodore interrupts his boss and benefactor. "Jimmy helped us launch the boat."

A flash of anger sparks across Burwell's face. Maybe Theodore was meant to keep up some ruse about Jimmy not being on the casino boat.

Theodore widens his stance. "I will not speak ill of the dead. He helped us, and now he is gone."

For some reason, that statement fills Burwell with relief. My initial assumption that he intended the storm to sink the boat and erase all trace of his sins bubbles to the surface.

"When I was here earlier, you mentioned having crews out looking for Leticia. I'm sure

Sheriff Harper would like the names of the men on those crews."

Burwell brightens. "Of course. I can get them for you now, if you'll take me out of these infernal manacles."

Erick nods, hands me a key, and I reluctantly free my first official collar.

He strides purposefully back toward his desk, glances at the top right drawer, wisely reconsiders, and retrieves a sheet of paper from his blotter. "Here. These are the names and phone numbers of the two contacts. They can provide the details of their searches. Believe it or not, Sheriff, I am heartbroken by the loss of Ms. Whitecloud. As your civilian liaison rightly assumed, we were more than business associates."

The upside of his brief speech is that now I know exactly the vibe he emanates when he's lying through his teeth. Although, I'm not quite sure which part is the lie. There'll be time to examine the memory later—in safety.

"Theodore, I will ask you to stand down. Miss Moon and the generous sheriff are free to come and go from the casino at will. We'll do nothing to impede their investigation, and offer such assistance as we can. Would this be agreeable, Sheriff?"

Erick nods, removes the handcuffs from Theodore, and pats the young man on the back.

"I'm keeping your gun, Teddy. And I'll send a deputy out to fingerprint both of you. Just to eliminate you from the prints found on the murder weapon."

Opening my mouth to protest, I luckily realize why Erick is lying. Now I have to hide my joy. He's purposely misleading them. Earlier, he told me plain as day that there were no fingerprints found on the weapon. Subterfuge. How exciting!

Burwell swallows with great effort. "Of course. As I said, Sheriff, we shall offer whatever assistance we can. Please have your deputy ask for me personally."

Erick nods. "Oh, I will."

As soon as he closes the driver's side door of the patrol car, I squeal with delight. "Did you see me slide across the desk!"

He chuckles and shakes his head. "I had my hands full with Teddy."

I press my palms against the dashboard, lean back into the seat, and gasp. "How can you call him Teddy? You heard his voice, right? I mean, it was like he stepped right out of a 1950s movie! That transatlantic accent. I can't believe him and Jimmy are related."

Erick slowly turns his head toward me as he simultaneously navigates across the parking lot. "Are you holding out on me, Moon?"

"Not intentionally. You're the one who lives here. I thought you knew."

"Who told you?"

"Jimmy. He said that when his son went to prison, his mom's sister moved away to avoid the scandal. She married into a clan in Canada, and Jimmy is the one who got Theodore this job."

"Wow. You were actually keeping quite a few things from me."

"Not important ones." My hand shoots over to his knee and I squeeze it reassuringly.

Erick rubs his left thumb along his jaw and stares straight ahead. "You don't think it's weird?"

"The job? I don't know. I don't have any cousins —that I know of." The thought gives me an uncomfortable chill and I push it away.

"Sure, but technically Jimmy worked for the competition. I'm not even sure I believe Burwell's story about cutting Leticia in on the profits. Why would he do that?"

"Maybe Leticia had something on him. She was always manipulating things behind the scenes. She probably got him the job because she knew she could control him."

He shakes his head. "I don't think so. The Council pushed her out for a reason. Why would they hire anyone she recommended?"

The high from the antics in Burwell's office is

194 / TRIXIE SILVERTALE

fading. "I don't know. Maybe she waited until after they hired him—"

"When someone on the inside could pass her incriminating information?" Erick glances at me from the corner of his eye. "Maybe Teddy getting the job was no coincidence either."

He has a point. His years of experience in law enforcement have their advantages. However, once I get home and access all my psychic powers in the privacy of my hidden apartment, I'm sure I'll find a connection that's escaping my five regular senses.

"You're awful quiet, Moon. Should I be concerned?"

"I'm mulling over the details. I'd prefer to be basking in the glory of my fantastic takedown, but someone's casting doubts on my open-and-shut theory."

"Didn't mean to burst your bubble. The only theory we have right now is that everyone's guilty until they're not."

"I couldn't agree more. But I was awesome."

He shakes his head and chuckles. "Aren't you always?"

CHAPTER 15

ERICK TURNS DOWN the alley next to my bookstore to drop me off, leans toward the passenger seat, and takes the liberty of an extra-long goodbye kiss. Fine by me.

"I need to get over to the station and assign a deputy to the casino before Burwell withdraws his offer."

"Copy that."

"Can I bring you dinner tonight?"

"You know me, I never say no to food."

He grins and chuckles. "Now we both have something to look forward to." Smiling, I innocently close the door of the cruiser. However, as I walk toward the shop, the full weight of his words sends my tummy into flip-flops. Geez. I'm the thing he's looking forward to!

The dopamine rush of his unconditional love, and the lingering pride of my kick-butt take down have me smiling from ear to ear as I march up the circular staircase.

When I catch sight of the firmly closed bookcase door, I stop on the thick carpets and a chill of concern rushes over me. I slowly turn in a full circle and search for unfamiliar energy.

Nothing blips on my psychic radar.

My concern grows as I tiptoe along the curved left arm of the mezzanine. My hand slides over the reassuring thick balustrade, while my senses carefully search every corner of the first floor.

By the time I reach the end, and have a vantage point all the way to the side door, an anomaly finally catches my attention.

The red glow has returned to the EXIT sign above the alley door.

Electricity! This crazy case has me so distracted, I completely forgot they had restored the electricity.

Breathing a sigh of relief, I trot toward the bookcase. As I pass the tall ladder, which slides along the rail beneath the highest shelf, a loud crash brings a fresh wave of panic washing over me.

A streak of tan bolts across the Rare Books Loft and crouches expectantly under an oak reading table.

"Robin Pyewacket Goodfellow! Not all of us have unlimited lives! One of these days you're going to scare the bejeezus out of me for the last time."

"Ree-ow." I'd like to believe that was his version of an apology, but, honestly, it sounds more like a condescending acknowledgment of my fragile humanity.

Before fear gets the best of me, I stoop to investigate the mess. Despite my frustration, history has taught me well. My spoiled feline rarely does anything on a whim.

Three books lie in a tumble on the carpet. "Let's see what you've put on my reading list today."

"*When the Rain Sings, After the Snow Melts,* and *Poison in the Parish.* Am I supposed to read all of these or is there some clever connection between the titles?"

The hellacious wildcat remains utterly silent.

"Great. You dump a stack of books and offer no further assistance."

"Reow." Can confirm.

Approaching the hidden apartment with some trepidation, I gently tug the candle handle. The bookcase door slides open, and I can't stop myself from shouting a little "woot" for electricity.

Ghost-ma hits me with an announcement as

soon as I cross the threshold. "Mitzy! I made a decision!"

"Seems like the left-field thing runs in the family, eh, Grams?"

"You crack me up, sweetie."

Stepping into the closet, I retrieve the pendant from a hook, and carefully cradle the amber stone containing my grandmother's spirit in my hand. "What did you decide?"

"I want to do it! Let's give that ritual a try. I have to get out of this thing. It's seriously crushing my style."

"Oh no. Anything but your style." My words are flippant, but my heart hurts when I entertain the possibility of life without her loving support. I struggle to remind myself that love isn't about limits and control—it's about freedom. "I support your decision, one hundred percent."

Grabbing my phone, I ring Silas.

"Good evening, Mitzy. How are you and your grandmother on this fine day?"

There's the Silas I know and love. "We're both doing well. How are you, Mr. Willoughby?"

"I too am well. Thank you for enquiring. How may I help?"

When I open my mouth to share the news, my throat tightens and I can't seem to get out the words. A stifled choke is all that spills forth.

"Has Isadora made her decision?"

"Mmhmm."

"She has chosen to proceed with my recommendation."

"Mmhmm."

Silas harrumphs. "I have the supplies at the ready and shall depart in a quarter of an hour."

Before ending the call, I manage to choke out a thank you.

Grams is quietly sniffling, and I'm eager to ignore the heavy emotional burden resting on my shoulders. "What should we do until he gets here?"

She sniffles. "Would you consider spending what could be my last hour on Earth planning your wedding?"

Shock grips me and I almost drop the necklace. "What are you talking about? I'm not getting married! Erick and I are taking things slow, remember?"

"Oh, no, sweetie. When you've been around as long as I have, and been married as many times as I have, you develop an instinct about these things. It may not be this year, or even next year, but it's going to happen. You two are meant to be."

I'm speechless.

She continues as though I've offered my whole-hearted support. "If something goes wrong, and I crossover, my only regret will be missing the happiest day of your life."

That sweet sentiment turns on my waterworks. "But you didn't, Grams! The happiest day of my life was when you popped into existence right in front of my face and nearly made me pee my pants! Living in this apartment and having my own personal ghost guide to psychic powers has been the single best thing in my entire life."

She cries. I cry. We're an after-school special full of emotions.

"Hey, I'm not saying I haven't thought about marrying Erick. And if it happens, I'm sure it will be a wonderful day. But when I'm a hundred and something years old, sitting on my porch in a rocking chair, the moment you appeared and transformed my life will easily remain at the top of the list."

She mumbles something lovey-dovey, and I agree, even though I can't understand the teary declaration.

"So, long story longer, if you want to spend your last moments on this plane of existence planning my wedding, then I say let's go for it!"

"Oh, my goodness! I don't know where to begin." She directs me to the adjoining printing museum, and I use the light from my phone to navigate around the Gutenberg press and up the stairs to the alcove she used for writing her memoirs, before an angry gypsy jammed her into the soul trap.

"Open that left-hand drawer on the bottom."

As the drawer slides open, my eyes widen and I burst out laughing. "Oh, Isadora! You naughty, naughty ghost."

"I'm not sure what you mean, dear."

I can so easily picture her with one hand on her curvy hip and the other clutching a strand of pearls.

"Back when I could pick things up, I may have borrowed a few bridal magazines from the stacks and innocently folded over the pages of things I thought you might like."

"You're insufferable!" Laughter grips me and the strength of her love warms my heart. "All right, let's do this." I scoop the stack of magazines from the drawer and spread them out on the desk. I may not agree with her choices, but that's nothing new.

The minutes slip away.

BING. BONG. BING.

"Silas!" The shout that could be our last in *unison* fills me with a cacophony of emotion.

Grabbing the amulet, I race down the stairs, out of the printing museum, and toward the alley. "Come in. Come in. Grams and I— Never mind. We're ready. Where do we do this?"

Silas enters carrying a small leather bag and an

202 / TRIXIE SILVERTALE

air of mystery that both intrigues and concerns. "I believe the apartment would provide the proper balance of privacy and nostalgia."

I lead the way as Pyewacket leaps down from wherever he was hiding and joins our small parade.

Silas takes his usual seat in the scalloped-back chair, while Pyewacket and I share the sofa.

"Unlike some of our previous workings, Mizithra, we must communicate carefully during this transmutation. I will need your help as we attempt to re-attach the tether that once held your grandmother to this place."

"Copy that. Whatever you need."

He then turns to Pye, smooths his bushy mustache with his thumb and forefinger, and wags his jowls. "There will be fire, my little friend. All will be controlled, but I must ask that you refrain from interrupting, even if it goes against your instincts."

Pyewacket settles back on his majestic haunches and squeezes his golden eyes closed with inestimable wisdom.

"Fire? Like actual fire, or magic fire?"

Silas lifts his saggy chin and prepares to lecture me.

"My bad. I mean, alchemical fire."

"Perhaps there is yet hope."

Grams whispers from the amulet tightly

clenched in my hand. "I'll never give up hope, sweetie."

A single tear trickles down my cheek. "I can't make it without my cheering section, Silas. You tell me what to do and I'll do it. Fire, walking on hot coals, whatever you need."

"You and your grandmother certainly share a flair for the dramatic. The instructions are simple. You will be required to trust. That is all."

Experience warns me I will regret not asking for clarification, but I'm eager to get underway.

My mentor places his tattered leather satchel on the coffee table and carefully unloads the contents.

First out of the bag is a shallow silver tray, similar in size to a pie plate, but more ornate.

Next a small circular mirror, a bottle of seemingly average water, and three various-sized mysterious vials.

Three? Why does that number give me *déjà vu?* Focus, Mitzy. No time for distractions.

"Please hand me the amulet."

Glancing down at the white knuckles on my right fist, my eyes widen. "Oh, I didn't realize I still had it."

"Indeed. Place it on the table next to the other items."

My right hand is so sweaty, I have to transfer

the pendant to my left and, as I reach toward the table, the strange tingling in my mood ring recurs. "Hey, I forgot to tell you!"

Silas harrumphs and shakes his head. "I must ask that you maintain decorum. There will be verbal exchanges during this process, but you must not upset the energies."

I gently place the amber stone on the coffee table and lean back like a scolded child. "Sorry. I thought it might be important."

"What is it that troubles you?"

"It's not trouble, exactly, but I've noticed it a couple times now. When the mood ring gets close to that necklace, there's a tingly thing that happens."

My helpful ghost blurts, "And tell him about the one time it floated."

"Right! And there was one time when the amulet actually floated off my chest for a second."

Silas leans back, steeples his fingers and begins rhythmically bouncing his chin on the tips of his pointers. "Perhaps this is the link we seek. The ring belonged to your grandmother, and, if memory serves, triggered your own psychic abilities."

"Yeah. That's exactly what happened. Could this be *the thing*, the thing that will keep her here?"

His milky-blue eyes water and he blinks back the emotion. "Time will tell. Are you both ready to begin?"

"I'm ready, Mitzy. Tell him. Tell him I've never been so ready for anything in my whole life."

Grams' exuberance lightens the mood and brings a much-needed smile to my face. "We're ready."

The aged alchemist draws in a long breath, and the ravages of time seem to melt away as his stooped shoulders square and his rheumy eyes brighten. "Let us begin."

He picks up the mirror and places it in the center of the silver pan and then removes the amber pendant from its chain.

As usual, I lean forward, bursting with anticipation and awe.

The stone rests on top of the mirror like a miniature display, as he uncorks the bottle of water, and gently pours it into the dish. Eventually, the amber is completely submerged, and a sharp odor reaches my nostrils. It almost burns, like rubbing alcohol. Maybe it's not pure water.

Silas opens the small blue vial and tips three nuggets of what appear to be gold into his palm. He meticulously places each tiny piece at the points of an invisible triangle in the water.

He takes the next vial, a deep green, uncorks it, and pours the viscous fluid directly in the center of the pan, on top of the amber. And finally he opens the last remaining vial, three times the size of the blue and green, pulls the cork, and pours a circle of salt around the pan. He then holds his right hand above the immersed pendant and snaps his fingers.

I gasp and lean back as flame ignites across the water. Before my eyes, the amber stone seems to be disintegrating or melting. "It's working! She's going to be free!"

Silas gazes across the blue-orange flames with an intensity that grips my soul. "Mizithra Achelois Moon, you must reach into the flame and grasp your grandmother's spirit as it seeps from its prison."

"You want me to put my hands in the fire?" I'm hoping I misheard.

His stoic face says it all.

I guess this is the trusting part. Leaning forward, I wait for the amber to recede further. Beneath the flame, I see a glow of a different kind, as the spirit of my precious grandmother bubbles to the surface.

"Now." His deep tone vibrates up from the floor.

I suck air into my lungs and prepare for the worst pain I can imagine as I thrust my hands into the living flame to scoop them around the forming ball of Ghost-ma energy.

There's no pain. My entire body feels as though it's floating. "I'm free!"

Her energy fills the pulsing orb in my hands as her spirit escapes the stone.

Suddenly, I'm gazing down on the scene. I see myself sitting across from Silas, with my hands in a bowl of fire. Wait! Am I my having an out-of-body experience? Am I the one who said, "I'm free?"

Even as I watch the scene unfold below me, I witness a furry feline rise up and place both of his large paws on my right shoulder.

In a snap, my point of view changes and I'm back inside my body.

The flames dissipate, my breathing returns to normal, and Silas leans back in his chair with a sigh of exhaustion. "We almost lost you. If not for the quick thinking of Pyewacket, you may have slipped away with your grandmother."

I'm so busy inspecting the flesh on my hands, for any sign that they spent the last few minutes plunged into flame, his comment barely registers. "What do you mean? With my grandmother? Oh no, I got distracted, didn't I? I was supposed to be concentrating on how much I love her, and the stupid fire stuff mesmerized me. I didn't find the link. I didn't hold—"

"You cannot bear this burden alone. We all knew the risks when we began the working. Equal measures success or failure, remember?"

"Sure, but I thought it was like 'four out of five

dentists' or 'sixty-five percent of the time it works every time.' I didn't think it would happen to us. I didn't think she would actually go."

Pye shoves his way under my elbow and into my lap. The weight of him sprawled across my legs is the only thing forcing me to accept this is reality and not a bad dream.

Silas quietly decants the liquid from the silver dish into an empty container from his satchel, packs up the rest of his supplies, and rises from the chair. "I will leave you to your grief. When you are ready to discuss the events of the day, or perhaps have an idea concerning how you wish to honor your grandmother, I will participate in that ceremony. I am sorry for your loss."

The all-to-familiar phrase sends me hurtling back in time.

That knock on the door of my dingy apartment. The envelope containing so much hope. The discovery of family.

Tipping onto my side, I curl my arms around my fur baby and weep as the montage of all montages plays in my mind.

A tiny piece of me is so grateful for all these memories, but the vast majority is broken beyond repair and knows there'll never be another truly happy day in my life.

I can't be sure how long I lie there in a pool of

sorrow and my own tears, but when the bell rings indicating a visitor at the alley door, I have no interest in answering.

Several seconds go by and my phone pings with a text message.

I don't have the strength to move my hand, let alone the courage to see who's reaching out.

The bell at the alley door rings again, and Pyewacket slinks away.

Moments later, the bookcase slides open and an energy I could sense anywhere steps into my apartment.

"Mitzy? What's wrong? I was worried when you didn't answer the door or your phone. And when your cat came down to let me in, that didn't help matters."

Erick sets two pizza boxes on the coffee table and the second they cover the chain that once held the cursed pendant, I sit up and shove them violently to the floor. "No." Reaching out, I grab the chain and clutch it to my chest.

He sits next to me, puts an arm around my shoulders, and kisses the top of my head. "Hey, I'm here. You can tell me. You can tell me anything."

His simple words and his caring touch reach through my pain. "She's gone. We tried to get her out of the amulet thingy, but—"

He touches the chain spilling out of my left

hand and speaks softly. "No one can take your memories, Mitzy. I can't begin to imagine what it was like to get to know your grandmother after she became a ghost. In fact, now that I'm saying it out loud, I can't even imagine ghosts to begin with, but that's not the issue. What I'm trying to say is, I know what it's like to lose people. And whether they're human or ghost, it hurts. Anyone who tells you different is lying. Time and action are the only things that ever helped me. Unfortunately, time runs at one speed for all of us, but you can take action whenever you want. If solving this case will help you cope, then I will move heaven and earth to help you any way I can."

The wounded child inside is struggling to bottle up all the emotions of losing her mother when she was eleven and now her beloved grandmother barely a decade later. But the amateur sleuth, and her ever-growing psychic powers, gets the upper hand. "You're right."

He smiles encouragingly.

The mood ring on my left hand seems like too much baggage right now. I walk to my grandmother's jewelry box, push the hidden latch, and slip the piece of history back into its resting place. I sniffle and swipe at my nose. "Grams loved catching bad guys as much as me. Let me get my head together, organize this murder wall, and let's lock up some bad guys for Grams!"

Erick hugs me close and wipes a tear from my cheek. "And not to overstep, but I think Isadora would like you to do that in heels."

Laughter and tears spill forth in equal measure. "You're not wrong."

CHAPTER 16

DESPITE THE LATE HOUR, Erick's suggestion that I process my grief with action is pure genius. Even though the act of selecting a crime-fighting outfit induces a fresh wave of tears, the end result is worth it.

Isadora would be proud. I am the living embodiment of a 1970s era female butt-kicker. Let's start from the bottom and work our way up, shall we? Platform suede boots. Hiphuggers with bell bottoms. A polyester top with stripes of harvest gold, edging a deep-V neckline. And, to top it all off, a pair of Riviera light-sensitive sunglasses that would make Diana Prince swoon. Plus, I tuck the infamous gun in the back of my waistband, hidden under my suede coat. My little secret.

When Erick opens the passenger-side door of

his patrol car, I feel like I've walked onto the set of *The Mod Squad.*

He jumps in and starts the engine. "Where to?"

"The safe house."

Erick looks at me and scrunches up his nose. "Maybe you better tell me what you're after. We don't have a safe house in Pin Cherry, per se."

Oh Icarus, once again you flew too high. I rephrase my request. "That sniveling busboy/server is hiding something. So take me to wherever you're keeping him."

"Actually, Paulsen thought the safest place for him was in a cell."

"How convenient. For once, I agree with her. Set him up in Interrogation Room One, and I'll stumble in like I've made a wrong turn. Let him think I'm his friend—and then I'll get him to spill his guts."

"Easy Starsky, or are you Hutch?"

"Whoa. I thought I was pulling off Angie Dickinson in *Police Woman.* No?"

He laughs a little too long as he eases the cruiser into a parking spot in front of the station. "Give me five minutes to put him in interrogation, and then the station is all yours."

I know he's breaking all the rules just to help me forget my troubles, but it makes me love him all the more. "Thank you. You really are the best boyfriend."

He chuckles as he slides out of the seat. "I have to step up my game. With Deputy Candy nipping at my heels, I don't want to jeopardize my ranking."

"Rude! I'm not interested in that man-child."

His broad shoulders shake with laughter as he disappears inside the building.

I check my phone and have to admit that I'll be lucky if I can give him three minutes. Plus, I notice my battery is dangerously low. Great. Total amateur move.

I last roughly three and a half minutes and then slide my "out of sight" self out of the vehicle.

If you've never walked in full-on 70s platform shoes, then you've missed an amazing slice of life. There is literally no way to motate without being seriously funky. I strut toward the front desk, and, before I can even open my mouth, Deputy Baird a.k.a. Furious Monkeys points over her shoulder toward the interrogation rooms.

I nod and toss her a period-correct response. "Groovy."

Shockingly, that gets direct eye contact and an arched eyebrow.

Smiling, I wink and offer her a finger gun.

Erick's office door is closed, but I'm willing to

bet he's not in there. If I were him, I'd be posted up in the observation room, with the speaker on.

Feigning a mid-conversation bumble, I stumble into Interrogation Room One as I call out over my shoulder, ". . . like I said, it's all in the shoes."

Turning toward the shocked face of Tripp Kenosha, I stop short and put a hand to my cheek. "Whoops! This clearly isn't the ladies' room."

He blinks, and recognition floods his features. "Hey, you're that Mitzy. From the boat, right?"

That sounds like an invitation to me. I pull out the chair opposite and strike a power pose. "That's right. What are you in for?"

He shakes his head. "No. No. I'm not in trouble. Remember? You brought me here. Like for safety, or whatever."

"I did? Right, that does sound like something I would do. What am I keeping you safe from?"

"James. The guy you asked me about on the boat."

As Scooby-Doo would say, ruh-roh. Taking a deep breath, I force myself not to pounce on his potential slip of the tongue. "You mean, Jimmy, Leticia's bodyguard?"

The color drains from his face like sand through an hourglass, and his Adam's apple bulges as he forces himself to swallow. "Yeah, you call him Jimmy. But he makes us all call him James."

"Cool. Cool. So you think Jimmy is the one who broke into your apartment and messed it up?"

He pulls his hands into his lap, and I can hear the nervous flick of his fingernails as he fidgets. "Totally. Everyone was so edgy."

"Sure. Who wouldn't be, man? The big boss lady fired someone, right?"

He straightens in his chair and makes another desperate gulp for oxygen. "Oh, I told you that part, I guess."

I slide my sunglasses down to the tip of my nose and lean across the table. "Yeah, you told me a lot of things, kid. I'm starting to wonder if any of them were true." The low, aching timbre of my voice is hard to maintain, and if I utter even one more word, I'm certain I'll start coughing. Better to keep quiet and maintain my intimidating pose.

It works. Tripp nearly crawls out of his skin, eager to say anything to please me. "I had to tell you that stuff. He paid me."

"Jimmy paid you to make him look guilty? Sounds a little freaky deaky. I have it on good authority that he was on the boat, and several eyewitnesses saw him helping Mr. Burwell into a small inflatable craft right before the sirens went off. Why would Jimmy—"

The young man is stock-still. If I hadn't seen him speaking earlier, I'd be concerned he was a mannequin. Something I'm saying is lighting a paralyzing fire of fear underneath his feet. Whew, try to say that five times fast. Focus, Mitzy.

Tripp's jaw quivers as he replies. "That was um, a slip of the tongue."

"Jimmy isn't the one paying you, is he?" Leaning back, I push my sunglasses in place, cross my arms, and smirk as the pieces fall into place. "Where's his son? Where's James? That was no slip of the tongue earlier. You said James and you meant James. You've got fifteen seconds, punk. Nobody knows I'm in here, and nobody's going to care what happens to you if you don't tell me what I want to know." I attempt to disguise the resulting cough from delving into the lower octaves of my vocal range with a bravado-filled scoff.

The kid's too terrified to notice and immediately spills his guts. "Yeah. Okay. You got me." He lifts his hands in the air. "James is the one who paid me and he also got that kid drunk, so he'd get fired. I don't know. I just did what I was told, because I was scared, you know? James has this whole list of people he's out to get. Did you know he was in prison?"

I've recovered my vocal abilities and I delve into my lower register one last time. "Oh, I know quite a lot of things. One thing I don't know, is the thing you're going to tell me right now. Where is James?"

A visible shiver shakes the kid's slight frame. "I don't know. I met him at an abandoned gas station one time. Down at the docks, by the train station one time. He moves around. He's super sketchy. Always thinks someone's following him."

As I unfold myself from the chair, the increased height added by my sweet platform boots gives me a boost of confidence. I figure stealing a move from a guy I admire is exactly what needs to be done. I rap my knuckles twice on the table and throw in a finger gun for good measure.

As soon as the door closes behind me, I gasp for air. A powerful arm reaches out from the observation room and pulls me inside. "Was that an audition for an all-female remake of *Starsky and Hutch*?" Erick's cheeks are red with laughter and I can imagine he very much enjoyed the show.

"You know what, my exceptional performance got us the break in the case we needed. So maybe you should show me a little more respect."

He puts his hands together in prayer-pose and bows repeatedly. "Yes, Your Highness. Yes, My Queen."

"Oh brother. That's enough. Let's get after it."

He wipes a hand over his mouth and nods. "Where are we headed? Docks?"

"Nope. Something about that abandoned gas station he mentioned seemed right. The docks are too exposed. James is going to need to lie low, and hiding out in a building everyone thinks is abandoned seems like the perfect plan."

Erick nods his agreement. "Until Moon and Harper bust the door down."

This comment catches me completely off guard, and I laugh so hard my sunglasses nearly fall off. "There's only room for one diva in this crime-fighting duo, Sheriff. Stay in your lane, gurrrrl."

He smiles, kisses my cheek, and leads the way outside. As I strut through the bullpen—again, unable to walk any other way—Deputy Candy jumps to his feet and makes a disturbing animal sound. My plan, ignore him completely.

Erick takes another approach. "Looks like you're ready for another assignment, Deputy. Make sure the Kenosha kid gets put back in lockup. He's no longer a witness. He's an accomplice, one way or another."

Deputy Candy's mouth is hanging open a bit and his eyes are still pasted on me. Erick snaps his fingers. "Now, Deputy. This isn't the academy, and this ain't a drill."

Finally, the creepy little copper hustles off to the interrogation room.

Due to the massive economic crisis that rocked the region after the shutdown of the iron ore mines, there's more than one abandoned gas station in Pin

Cherry Harbor. However, one of my previous in-vestigations revealed that only one of those dilapi-dated service stations is still owned by the tribe. Erick and I head directly to that location.

"So when we get there, you can kick the door down and I'm gonna say something like, 'My dad saved your life, and this is how you repay me, James?'"

Erick shakes his head. "Not exactly. Since this is real life, and not one of your mind movies, you're going to wait in the car. I'm going to check the perimeter for signs of life, and then I'll call for backup."

Crossing my arms, I push out my lower lip and pout.

"Don't try to distract me with your sexy lips, Moon. We're going to follow procedure, and that's final."

"Fine. But don't come crying to me when your plan utterly fails. The only thing we have going for us is the element of surprise. Parking and checking perimeter stuff is just going to give James time to get away."

"Easy, Pepper. We'll get it." Erick parks just be-yond the line of sight of the station, crouches low, and ducks into the alley next to the abandoned building to initiate his perimeter check.

Every fiber of my being wants to kick in that

front door. I mean, the size of these platform boots—

The passenger door of the cruiser yanks open, and a hand covers my mouth.

Instantly I struggle, but at the same moment a heavy chemical scent floods into my nose and mouth. Crap balls! Is that chloro—?

When I come to, I'm in a 6 x 8 wooden shed, and there's weak artificial light seeping through the cracks between the boards on the left side. How long was I out? Is that a streetlight? Before I discern my captor's identity, I sense dampness in the air and hear the faint lapping of waves. Sounds like the docks. Apparently, I made the wrong choice when I picked the gas station.

"Good. You're awake. "

My eyes flip open and my mouth hangs loose.

"It's not what you think. I'm trying to keep you safe."

"Isn't that what a murderer would say, Jimmy?"

"Look, I knew that Kenosha kid would crack. Once I saw you and the sheriff looking around the gas station, I didn't want you to get yourself killed."

"Again, sounds a bit like a murderer's line. You didn't want me to get myself killed, because you wanted to kill me. What's going on, Jimmy?"

He stands, and, as the bearlike man walks toward me, all the cool of my platform boots evaporates.

Desperate to distract, I throw out my only pitch. "Where's Tom Sawyer, or should I say James?"

Jimmy stops in his tracks. "So you know?"

I have no idea what he's talking about, but at this point it's probably best to act like I know more than I do, and see what I can get out of him. "Yeah. Of course I know. Why do you think we were at the gas station looking for James?"

Jimmy sighs, and his massive shoulders curve forward. He shuffles back to the tattered campstool and drops onto it with a huff. "I hated to think it might be true, but he was never the same, you know, after prison."

"That's not your fault. Why didn't you get him help?"

"That's not our way."

"What's your part in this, Jimmy? Did you kill Leticia?"

He covers his mouth with a broad hand, and his eyes darken. "It's a choice no one should face. He's my son. He was done wrong, and I let it happen."

"So you went along with his crazy revenge plot because you had a guilty conscience?"

"A life for a life. The balance must be restored."

I lean forward to get up from the chair, but

Jimmy shows me the gun. "I took this back. Thanks for taking care of it for me."

Touché. "Jimmy, your son didn't lose his life. I'm not saying it was fair that he went to prison for someone else's crime, but it happens."

"He's different now. Hard. Vengeful."

"Jimmy, who killed Leticia?"

"I thought Burwell was setting me up." His stoic features crease with pain and suppressed emotions shake his shoulders.

The truth hits me right in the psychic gut. "I hate to say it, but James has to pay for what he's done."

Jimmy stands up in anger and waves the gun dangerously. "He already paid. Don't you see? He already paid!"

The large man is as agitated as a caged animal, and I'm running out of options. "Where are my sunglasses?"

"What? I don't know what you're talking about, Moon."

Good. Maybe they fell off when Jimmy grabbed me outside the gas station. Maybe Erick found them and he's looking for me right now.

Jimmy's mood shifts. "I'm sorry about the way this worked out. You shouldn't have stuck your nose in."

"Me? You asked me to help you, remember?

You're the one who pulled me into this. My blood is on your hands, Jimmy. You'll have to look my father in the eye and tell him you didn't keep your promise."

I'm spitballing in a devil-may-care bid to stay alive, but something in my words hits home. Jimmy's anger evaporates, and he slumps onto the stool.

A tense silence hangs thick between us.

The loose rope around my wrists seems as though it were an afterthought. I easily slip my right hand from the knots and inch it toward the pocket containing my phone.

Jimmy's head is down, and he pays me no mind.

My hand eases into the suede pocket. I check the volume button to make sure it's off, press the home key twice, slide my hand toward the top of the phone and pray to the ghost of my dearly departed grandmother that I tapped Sheriff Harper's name on my list of favorites.

The glow from my pocket catches Jimmy's attention. "You shouldn't have done that." He launches out of the camp chair, as I shout as much information as I can. "Jimmy. Docks. Boathouse—"

His hand is around my throat, and I'm worried this could be the end.

He points the gun in his left hand directly at my chest. "Shut it off."

The deathly quiet whisper causes me to quake

with fear. As I reach into my pocket to retrieve the phone and carry out my captor's instructions, I discover the battery died.

Waving the phone wildly with my right hand and choking for air causes enough confusion that Jimmy releases his hold on my neck. I hunch forward in an overly dramatic, but real, attempt to catch my breath and, when I rise up, I bring the thick sole of my disco boot right into his disco b—

He crumples forward with a painful groan, and I twist the gun from his hand. The door of the shed bursts open and I can't believe Erick has already found me. "Erick! Over here."

"Wrong again."

The prison-hardened form of James Blackburn fills the doorway with dread. "I had three names on my list. And I just added a fourth."

It doesn't take a genius to figure out that the new name is mine. I fire a warning shot that actually connects.

James yelps, pulls his weapon and returns fire.

I'd like to say my whole life flashes before my eyes, but the only thing I see is my eleven-year-old face crying bitter tears as my babysitter tells me my mother is dead.

There's an impact, a groan, and a heavy crash.

Consciousness slips away, as I whisper, "I'm sorry, Erick."

CHAPTER 17

REGAINING AWARENESS IN THE AMBULANCE, my eyes struggle to focus. The sheriff angles over me with concern, and a few strands of enticingly out-of-place hair fall over his eye and beg to be touched.

The paramedic shines a bright penlight in each of my eyes and announces, "She's coming around, Harper."

The man named "Harper" leans in.

I smile up at the intense blue-grey eyes and whisper, "What's your first name, Harper?"

His eyes widen. "It's me, Erick. Don't you recognize me?"

"I'd like to. What do you have in mind, *Erick?*"

He leans back and wipes a hand across his brow as he turns away. "Is it amnesia? Did she hit her head? I thought you said she only had two cracked ribs. This seems more serious. Take another look at her."

Harper moves out of the way and the EMT takes his place. "Miss Moon, do you know what day it is?"

A sly smile spreads across my face as I tilt my head and peer around the concerned medical professional. "Yeah, it's the day I *gotcha*, Sheriff Harper!"

Erick gently pushes the paramedic out of the way and brazenly kisses my smirking mouth. "Not funny, Moon. Not funny at all. Never do that to me again." His cheeks puff out as he exhales with relief. "I was running down that dock— I heard the gunshots—" He puts a hand over his mouth and shakes his head. "You were crumpled underneath Jimmy. There was blood everywhere."

Reaching out, I grip his hand and squeeze hard. "Sorry. The last thing I remember is James returning fire. I didn't mean to scare you. Wait! Am I shot? Why was there blood?"

He leans back and squares his shoulders. "Jimmy's dead. He took a bullet for you. I thought they were going to be able to save him, but he didn't even make it into the ambulance. The last thing he said was, 'Tell Jacob we're even.' Do you know what he means by that?"

My chest tightens and my cracked ribs ache

with pain, but it's nothing compared to the hurt in my heart. "Yeah, it's between him and my dad. I don't think I should say."

"Understood." He rubs my hand and squeezes my fingers. "You scared me. I'm still not clear about what happened. Did James grab you out of the cruiser?"

Although I'm in an ambulance nursing a painful injury, I can't keep the superior grin from my face. "Oh, you mean when you left me in the patrol car for my own safety?"

His shoulders droop, and he groans. "You're never gonna let me live that down, are you?"

"Not on your life. It was Jimmy who grabbed me. He said he was trying to keep me safe. Then James showed up, started threatening me, and shooting his mouth off about collecting on debts. I'm ninety-eight percent sure James is the one who killed Leticia, and I kinda think that Jimmy knew all about it. Why would he allow that?"

Erick's expression darkens. "We'll never know for sure. James will survive his injuries, though. You only grazed his shoulder, but he cracked his skull pretty good when I tackled him." There's a satisfied tone in Erick's voice.

"Ooooh, nobody messes with your girl."

He shakes his head. "I'd love for every criminal to politely surrender and calmly hop into my patrol car, but that's not how it usually goes. Once they patch him up, though, I'll have him in an interrogation room."

"Yeah, there's something not quite right. He said he had three names on his list, and I was number four."

"Who said that?"

Making the mistake of taking a deep breath sends a sharp pain spiking through my torso. "Yikes! Remind me not to breathe, or anything. Are they gonna put me in a cast?"

The paramedic leans around Erick. "No, Miss. You suffered a blunt chest wall injury. My on-scene assessment indicates possible fracture of ribs seven and eight. I've started an IV with an analgesic for the pain. They'll x-ray to confirm at the emergency room."

"And then a cast?"

"Not for simple fractures. They'll wrap your torso to restrict movement, if you request it. But you'll likely leave with only a scrip for more painkillers and some duty restrictions."

Staring at the needle in the back of my hand gives my tummy a swirl. "I forgot your question, Erick."

"What were you saying about a list?"

"Oh, right. When James blasted into the boathouse, he said he had three names on his list—

Pyewacket! Three Fruity Puffs left in the bowl. Three books knocked off the shelf. That cat is a genius!"

"Is she normally like this, Harper?" The EMT scowls with concern.

"Pretty much." Erick chuckles. "You were saying."

"Right. Then he said mine would be the fourth. We know Leticia was one of the names, and it sure seemed like he was setting up his dad to take the fall for her murder, so maybe Jimmy was name number two. Do you think Burwell was the third name? Or could it be that Tripp Kenosha kid?"

The sheriff shakes his head. "No idea. There's a deputy with him in the emergency room. As soon as they patch up his shoulder, we'll bring him in and get the rest of the story. He's got nothing to lose. He's going back to prison one way or another. I can't see why he wouldn't tell us the truth."

"Copy that. Now get me out of this meat wagon and let's get over to the station."

Erick chuckles. "Are you refusing medical treatment, Miss Moon?"

"Nice call back, Harper. I'm not refusing it, I'm postponing it. Let's solve this case, and then I'll get my ribs wrapped."

He turns to conduct a hushed exchange with the paramedic, and they agree to let me have my way. The ambulance turns around on Main Street and drops us at the sheriff's station.

As we walk in the front door, it feels like high noon at the O.K. Corral. I can almost hear myself saying, "S'cuse me, I need to shoot some people." Or whatever Wild West gunfighters would say before they dished out justice.

Deputy Paulsen meets us in the middle of the bullpen, and for a split second a look of admiration flashes across her face when she sees me, but she instantly replaces it with a takeaway. "I told you to leave it to the professionals, Moon. You'll never learn."

There it is again, a hint of esteem. Instantly covered with a snarl of her lips, but I swear she's impressed.

"We got Blackburn in two, Sheriff. He's been informed of his rights and the tape is rolling."

"Thanks, Paulsen." Erick walks tall toward the interrogation rooms, and I stop to slip into the observation room sandwiched between them. He pauses, looks over his shoulder and smiles. "If your ribs are up to it, I'd like you to join me in two, Moon. I think you've earned it."

"Wow! Thanks, Sheriff. I'll have to remember to crack my ribs more often."

Concern clouds his features, and he reaches toward me. "Please don't."

The warm flush of love colors my cheeks, and I struggle to get myself under control as we enter the interrogation room.

Erick steps into the far corner and offers me the chair. I shake my head and scowl at the infamous James Blackburn. "Surprised to see me alive?"

His lips curve with clear disdain for me, and everything I represent.

The pain on my right side prevents me from taking in enough air for increased volume or lengthy soliloquies. No worries. Short and to the point will work just fine. "Was killing your father always part of the plan?"

He maintains perfect control over his external expression, but the flush of satisfaction that I sense beneath the surface sickens me.

"That seems like a yes. I'm not sure how much you know about me, James, but I'm real good at getting to the bottom of stories." I have to pause and take another shallow breath. "The deeper you hide it, the quicker I find it. I know you killed Leticia Whitecloud, I saw you kill your father, and you told me there were three names on your list." One more little gasp. "Care to share that final name?"

His jaw clenches, and he makes no verbal reply, but the little tricks Silas taught me to grab something from the ether for that split second it exists in the subject's consciousness comes in handy.

"Theodore? Interesting."

The careful disinterest vanishes, and James leans back in shock and awe. "You're like the Raven. The stories are true."

I don't know exactly what he means, but I'm deeply concerned that he might be referencing my still-secret extrasensory abilities. Time to steer this boat back into the slip. ASAP. "Why would you need to kill your cousin, James? I get that you were out to right the wrongs of the people who betrayed you, but why him?"

His eyes offer silent agreement.

"Obviously you blamed your father for not standing up to Leticia, but why Theodore? What's his role in all of this?"

James' entire aura shifts. Before I could only feel blocks and resistance, now it suddenly feels as though I've turned my ship downstream and the water is pushing me forward with ease.

"Theodore is not my cousin. Just one more of my father's lies. He's my half-brother. Can you guess the union that brought him into this world, bird girl?"

Crossing my arms, I fix James with a pitiful glare. "I'd say Jimmy got Leticia pregnant long before he ever met your mother. They sent Theodore to be raised by an auntie and you grew up believing he was your cousin." I have to pause for air. Hopefully, he interprets it as a dramatic break. "Theodore committed whatever crime you went to jail for, and that was when you discovered his true lineage. Leticia's power and influence trumped your father's, and you took the fall. How am I doing?"

His dark-brown eyes flash with equal measures of hatred and surprise. "Quite well, for an outsider. Who told you this tale?"

"You did, James."

The hatred in his eyes evaporates, and for the first time I see pulses of fear flickering through the muscles of his face.

"What did Theodore do? And why did you have to pay for it?"

The powerful shoulders he inherited from his father slump as the last vestiges of defiance crumble. "Teddy doesn't like girls. If you know what I mean."

I nod. "And what does Theodore's sexual preference have to do with all of this?"

"Some of the guys found out. They jumped him. But he's strong. All the Blackburns are strong."

"So Theodore got the upper hand?"

"He did. One of the boys died from his injuries. The elders wanted to keep it quiet. No one believed Teddy beat down all five of them alone. The White-cloud woman told my father he must choose."

Erick steps forward and puts a hand on James' shoulder. "Jimmy chose his eldest son, right?"

Initially James shrugs, but his defenses are gone. He nods and his lips press into a fine line.

I don't understand the significance, but clearly born in wedlock does not outrank firstborn in the Blackburn clan.

James finally shows a morsel of regret. He hangs his head and his voice is barely a whisper. "He threw me away. He never even visited me in prison. You would treat a dog better."

My ribs are killing me and I need to wrap this up and get some pain meds. "I'm not gonna pretend I understand what you're going through, James. And I know Leticia was a hard woman. Your father probably thought you'd be out in a couple years on good behavior."

James gazes up with a wry smile twisting his mouth. "That's exactly what my lawyer told me. But Leticia wouldn't take the chance. She thought I'd make trouble for her precious Teddy if I got out. And the longer she left me in there, the more right she was. If Burwell hadn't messed with the radio, and set us up to die out on the lake, Teddy would already be joining his conniving mother."

Erick paces around the table and stands next to me. "So you killed Leticia Whitecloud, you killed

Jimmy Blackburn, and you planned to kill Theodore? Is that right?"

James nods. "Burwell was supposed to be the third, not Jimmy. I made the plan with Burwell and Teddy, but I was gonna tie up loose ends so that rat Teddy wouldn't turn on me again. 'Course he turned on me and tried to kill me in the tornado before I had a chance to take care of him. Once a rat, always a rat." His chin juts out and his bravado has returned. "I wanted my father to go to prison for someone else's crime. The bullet was meant for her." He juts his proud chin at me. "But, sure. Give me a sheet of paper, or whatever you want. I'll sign a confession."

"Revenge isn't as satisfying as you imagined, is it, James? Or should I say Tom Sawyer?"

He doesn't answer with words, but the blast of regret that hits my extrasensory antennae is the only answer I need.

Sheriff Harper turns off the recording device and motions for me to step into the hall.

Glancing at the hand where my mood ring usually resides, a claircognizant knowing bubbles to the surface. "The three thing was Leticia, Burwell, and Theodore—the three conniving criminals, not the list of victims. Still, Pyewacket rules."

"So, your cat gets hunches, too?"

I attempt to chuckle, but a shooting pain stabs through my torso.

His hand is instantly on my shoulder. "I'm gonna send someone out to pick up Burwell and Theodore. I'll have a lot of paperwork to process. Deputy Paulsen is going to take you to the ER now." He presses a finger to my lips. "Nope. No argument."

The adrenaline has definitely faded and the pain in my ribs can no longer be ignored. "Fine. You win."

He sighs. "No one won today." He gestures to Paulsen, and she grunts something as she waddles toward the door.

"I'll let your dad know where you are, and I'll see you later." He leans forward and kisses my cheek.

CHAPTER 18

AFTER TWO DAYS IN BED, hopped up on pain meds, I can't take it anymore. My dreams have been filled with memories of Grams, nightmares about being snatched, and longing to leave all the pain—physical and emotional—behind.

Maybe Pyewacket shouldn't have intervened and kept me grounded? Maybe it would've been better if I had crossed over with Grams and not had to feel this emptiness and survivor's guilt.

As I trudge down to make coffee, Erick's words echo in my head: time and action, time and action.

I wish my psychic powers included time travel, but that's probably slightly outside the realm of possibility. The action option seems most doable right now.

Maybe I can't change history, but hopefully I

can tip the future in my favor. I'm going to clean myself up, get an enormous basket of daisies, and invite Chayce down to the bookshop.

There. That should distract me from my pity party for a little while.

The rescheduled Midsummer Bonfire is tonight. It's no longer the actual solstice, and it's no longer a celebration. This new event is a memorial for the lives lost during what is being called the Superstorm of the Century. The residents of Pin Cherry were shaken to their core by the destruction of the library, but they are resilient. The larger tragedy is the way the twister's destruction forever scarred the families of those we lost.

The memorial gives us all a chance to speak the names of the departed and stand together in support of healing. My own heart is irreparably shredded after the unsuccessful alchemy and the loss of Ghost-ma.

Erick says he understands what I'm going through, and I'm sure he thinks he does. But the gaping hole that Grams lovingly filled in my heart feels like it will never be the same. The only bright spot in my day is the arrival of Chayce.

"I can't believe it! There's a whole giant basket of daisies. It's so cool. Do you need me to help you make another wreath?"

I smile into her warm brown eyes. "I think I remember, but if I get stuck you've got my back, right?"

She schools her features into what I'm sure she thinks is a serious adult expression. "Yeah. That's our deal."

Her father gazes around the bookshop and smiles. "Mitzy, would you mind if I poke around in the books while you two play with daisies?"

"Of course not. Make yourself at home. And if you find anything you like, it's yours. No charge."

He shakes his head. "Nothing doing. You saved my little girl's life. The least I can do is pay for a book if I find one that catches my eye."

"Suit yourself. We'll be down by the water." As we approach the side door, a jealous feline blocks my path.

"You have to stay inside. It's not a punishment. Some people are frightened of you, Pye."

Chayce switches the basket of flowers from her left hand to her right. "Can I pet him?"

Shrugging my shoulders, I crouch. "Let me check." I lean close to one of his tufted ears and whisper, "I need you to stay inside in case . . . In case Grams . . . Don't make me say it. Oh, and please let this little girl pet you."

"Reow." Can confirm.

"The boss says it's all right."

Her eyes light up and she leans toward his large

head. Pyewacket lets her scratch his head and even touch one of his ear tufts, but when she moves to scratch under his chin, he gives a soft hiss.

She jumps back in fright. "Is he gonna bite me?"

"Of course not. There's a cut on his chest. He was probably worried you'd bump it and hurt him. He's sort of a big baby."

"RE-OW!" Game on! Pyewacket launches over our heads and disappears up the circular staircase.

Her eyes are wide as saucers as she retrieves her basket. "Does he have superpowers? I've never seen a kitty jump that high!"

Truth be told, she's not far off on the super-power stuff. "Oh, Pyewacket has many secrets. Can you sit tight one minute? I forgot something upstairs."

She nods, sits down with her flowers and begins arranging the blooms by size.

I hustle up to the apartment, retrieve the mood ring from the jewelry box, and slip it in my pocket as I walk back to Chayce. I want to have that touch-stone with me during the ceremony. "Let's get out-side and make these wreaths."

Chayce braids a wreath for herself, one for her mother, and one for her father.

I make a wreath for myself, which she insists I wear, and then I make one more for my grandmother. Everyone is encouraged to make remembrance wreaths, and even though I didn't technically lose Grams in the storm, it all feels like part of the same enormous disaster.

Her dad arrives and shows me the book in his hand. "Do you think she'd like it if I read her *The Secret Garden?*"

"She'll love it."

He takes her down to the bonfire, and I hang in the deepening shadows.

When the evening's events begin, the festive energy of last weekend has been replaced with solemn words, gratitude to first responders, and thoughts and prayers for the families who lost loved ones and homes.

Nimkii recovered the chainsaw sculpture of the sun from the shores of the island. The somewhat dry artwork is back atop a new mound of driftwood, debris, and even planks from some of the lost vessels.

The mayor sets fire to the pyramid of wood, and as the pyre crackles a single voice rises in song. The always-full-of-surprises Twiggy is singing a beautiful funeral aria in a Scandinavian language I can't place. Her voice rings out crisp, clear, and full of heartache as the notes float across the great lake. Individuals and families approach the shore and toss their flower wreaths into the swash.

As I stumble toward the waves, I'm thankful Erick had official business, and I'm on my own. I don't need an audience for an ugly cry like this. I toss my crown of daisies into the lapping waves and send a final thought message into the void.

Myrtle Isadora Johnson Linder Duncan Willamet Rogers, you are the single greatest thing to ever happen to me. No matter how long I remain on this earth, I can honestly say I will never, and could never, love anyone as much as I loved you. I promise to take care of your precious Mr. Cuddlekins. And I vow to make sure he's buried next to you in the cemetery, but I secretly hope he never runs out of lives. I'll think of you every day. And I swear I will wear stupidly high heels at least once a month. They're not going to know what hit them on the other side of the veil. Give 'em hell, Grams.

Bending, I scoop up some cold water and splash it on my tear-streaked face. My submerged tennis shoes are soaked through and the sensation reminds me of the day of the storm, when I grabbed the red heart-shaped agate.

As I push my right hand into the pocket of my encore skinny jeans to feel if the stone is still there, my finger slips into the mood ring and it burns with an undeniable message. Pulling the hand toward me, I see my beautiful grandmother in her burgundy couture, swirling proudly in the mist. For a moment, I can almost hear her voice.

Wait.

I've never been able to hear things in the ring before.

It can't be.

I must be hallucinating.

"Not hallucinating, sweetie. I'm upstairs."

I spin around so quickly, I lose my balance and splash into the water. Looking up to the windows of my apartment, I gasp when I catch sight of a familiar ghost whizzing back and forth.

That's it. I've totally lost it. I'm having all kinds of psychic hallucinations—

Strong arms pull me from the water and brush the hair back from my face. "Hey, I asked Paulsen to take over at the station. I wanted to make sure you were okay." He touches my cheek. "I know today was hard for you. No one can ever replace your grandmother, but I want you to know I'm willing to spend the rest of my life trying."

I'm sure whatever he is saying is super sweet, but all I can see is a ghost dancing around in my window as though she's possessed. "I can't—" There are no words.

I rush across the beach, down the alley, and through the side door. As soon as my foot hits the floor of the bookshop, time stops.

It's not a hallucination. I am surrounded by the most loving energy I've ever felt in my life, and my grandmother's voice.

"I thought I lost you. We thought you crossed over. I mean, we agreed— But when the thing ended and you were gone—"

Her ethereal finger moves to hush my lips. She can't fully take corporeal form, so it's like the touch of an angel on my skin. "The ritual worked, sweetie. You and Silas freed me from that infernal pendant prison and you kept me here. Your love kept me on this side. The transition was rough, and I couldn't communicate with you. I was so discombobulated—"

The side door wrenches open, Erick takes one look at me hugging midair and an enormous smile cracks his face. "Isadora? You had us all worried sick."

She rushes toward him, and goosebumps flare on his bare arms.

"She's here. She didn't cross over. Isn't it fantastic? Now she'll be able to see all the important days in my life. There were so many things I thought I'd never get—"

Erick pulls me close and water soaks into his thin T-shirt. He kisses me softly and whispers, "I have some very special days planned, Moon. I'm happy to know your grandmother will be there."

All the week's stress and horror evaporate from my body as I collapse into his arms.

Grams swirls around and shouts, "Special days! You know what that means, dear!"

As Erick gently scoops me up and carries me toward the circular staircase, the last thing I remember is Ghost-ma loudly humming the wedding march, like a maniacal automaton on a cursed carnival ride.

Leave it to Grams to get the cart so far ahead of the horse we're all running to catch up!

End of Book 14

A NOTE FROM TRIXIE

Grams is back, baby—and another case solved! I'll keep writing them if you keep reading . . .

The best part of "living" in Pin Cherry Harbor continues to be feedback from my early readers. Thank you to my alpha readers/cheerleaders, Angel and Michael. HUGE thanks to my fantastic beta readers who continue to give me extremely useful and honest feedback: Veronica McIntyre, Margery Tipton, and Nadine Peterse-Vrijhof. And big "small town" hugs to the world's best ARC Team – Trixie's Mystery ARC Detectives!

As always, this book would not be the same without the edits of Philip Newey. Thank you for helping me realize that "motivate" is not a form of movement! I'd also like to give a whirlwind of gratitude to Brooke for her tireless proofreading! Any errors are my own.

Shout out to Morgan for firearms and radio protocol consulting.

FUN FACT: I was shopping at one end of a mall when a tornado ripped open the opposite end!

My favorite line from this case: She cries. I cry. We're an after-school special full of emotions. ~ Mitzy and Grams

I'm currently writing book fifteen in the Mitzy Moon Mysteries series, and I think I may just live in Pin Cherry Harbor forever. Mitzy, Grams, and Pyewacket got into plenty of trouble in book one, *Fries and Alibis*. But I'd have to say that book three, *Wings and Broken Things*, is when most readers say the series becomes unputdownable.

I hope you'll continue to hang out with us.

Trixie Silvertale (June 2021)

Mitzy Moon Mysteries 15

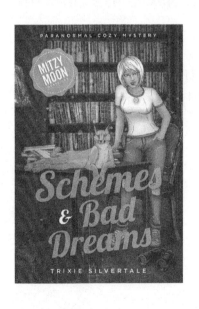

A blast from the past. A dangerous decision. This time, our psychic sleuth becomes the victim . . .

Mitzy Moon loves her new home town. But when history comes calling, she's tempted by distant memories and forced to reconsider. Now her sudden disappearance could be an impromptu road trip . . . or something more sinister.

Mitzy seems to have fallen off the map, but her

boyfriend, the handsome sheriff, continues to receive playful texts from the absentee heiress. Meanwhile, her entitled feline, Ghost-ma, and a powerful alchemist suspect foul play. Mitzy's captor may have control of her phone, but he's underestimated his prey.

Can Mitzy outsmart her jailer, or will her story be laid to rest?

Schemes and Bad Dreams is the fifteenth book in the hilarious paranormal cozy mystery series, Mitzy Moon Mysteries. If you like snarky heroines, supernatural misfits, and a splash of romance, then you'll love Trixie Silvertale's crooked caper.

Buy *Schemes and Bad Dreams* to flip the script on a kidnapper today!

Grab yours here!
readerlinks.com/l/861835

Scan this QR Code with the camera on your phone. You'll be taken right to the Mitzy Moon Mysteries series page. You can easily grab any mysteries you've missed!

Once you're in the Club, you'll also be the first to receive updates from Pin Cherry Harbor and access to giveaways, new release announcements, behind-the-scenes secrets, and much more!

Scan this QR Code with the camera on your phone. You'll be taken right to the page to join the Club!

THANK YOU!

Trying out a new book is always a risk and I'm thankful that you rolled the dice with Mitzy Moon. If you loved the book, the sweetest thing you can do (*even sweeter than pin cherry pie à la mode*) is to leave a review so that other readers will take a chance on Mitzy and the gang.

Don't feel you have to write a book report. A brief comment like, "Can't wait to read the next book in this series!" will help potential readers make their choice.

★★★★★

Leave a quick review HERE
https://readerlinks.com/l/1779034

★★★★★

Thank you kindly, and I'll see you in Pin Cherry Harbor!

More to come!

MAGICAL RENAISSANCE FAIRE
MYSTERIES

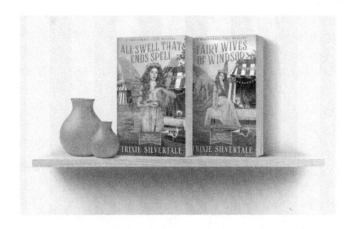

Explore the world of Coriander the Conjurer. A fortune-telling fairy with a heart of gold!

Book 1: **All Swell That Ends Spell** – A dubious festival. A fatal swim. Can this fortune-telling fairy herald the true killer?

Book 2: **Fairy Wives of Windsor** – A jolly Faire. A shocking murder. Can this furtive fairy outsmart the killer?

MYSTERIES OF MOONLIGHT MANOR

Join Sydney Coleman and her unruly ghosts, as they solve mysteries in a truly haunted mansion!

Book 1: **Moonlight and Mischief** – She's desperate for a fresh start, but is a mansion on sale too good to be true?

Book 2: **Moonlight and Magic** – A haunted Halloween tour seem like the perfect plan, until there's murder...

Book 3: ***Moonlight and Mayhem*** – An unwelcome visitor. A surprising past. Will her fire sale end in smoke?

ABOUT THE AUTHOR

USA TODAY Bestselling author Trixie Silvertale grew up reading an endless supply of Lilian Jackson Braun, Hardy Boys, and Nancy Drew novels. She loves the amateur sleuths in cozy mysteries and obsesses about all things paranormal. Those two passions unite in her Mitzy Moon Mysteries, and she's thrilled to write them and share them with you.

When she's not consumed by writing, she bakes to fuel her creative engine and pulls weeds in her herb garden to clear her head (*and sometimes she pulls out her hair, but mostly weeds*).

Greetings are welcome:
trixie@trixiesilvertale.com

BB bookbub.com/authors/trixie-silvertale

f facebook.com/TrixieSilvertale

O instagram.com/trixiesilvertale